The Trouble wi

Phyllis Pittman

Other Works
By Phyllis Pittman

Pony Tales: Night Mischief

Fairhope Anthology: Second in a Series
(Co-authored with the Fairhope Writers Group)

Original Fairhope Guidebook: A Walking Tour
(Co-authored with the Fairhope Writers Group)

www.phyllispittman.com

The Trouble with Grits . . .

The Trouble with Grits . . .

A Novel in Short Stories

PHYLLIS PITTMAN

Serendipity Press

www.serendipitypress.org

This is a work of fiction. All incidents and dialogue, and all characters, with the exception of some historical figures, are products of the author's imagination and are not to be construed as real. In all other respects, any resemblance to persons living or dead is entirely coincidental.

Published in the United States by Serendipity Press, Fairhope, Alabama.

ISBN 978-1-7323174-2-0

Ebook ISBN 978 1 7323174-1-3

First Edition: June 2018

Cover Design by Elise Johns

Cover art by Bill McCracken

For my family who have always encouraged and believed in me, especially my mother and father, who are looking down from Eternity and still cheering me on. For dear friends who have nudged, prodded, read, and stood firm.

Phyllis Pittman

"Don't he look natural?" Aunt Lavinia proclaims, staring into the mahogany box that holds the flesh and bones that used to hold my father. "Why do people say that?" barks Aunt Helen. "Who the hell looks natural when they're dead?"

"Hush," says Aunt Lavinia, glancing quickly over to where I stand in the corner placing a bouquet of white and red carnations on a table. Her distress increases when I clap my hand over my mouth. "He looks good," she says, trying to fix Aunt Helen's outburst.

"He looks dead, I imagine," Aunt Helen says just as loudly, ignoring her sister's efforts to shush her. Helen is stone blind and makes up for it in decibel level. "When I die," she continues, "I want the undertaker to put me in upside down, so everybody can kiss my . . ."

"Helen!"

"Butt," she finishes smugly.

There is no help for it now. The laughter bubbles out of me as Aunt Tiny and Aunt Lavinia each grab an arm and try to move their sister down the hall where they think she can do less harm.

Much of Covington and Smith counties have gathered here to mourn my father. This is far less impressive when you realize that my relatives make up most of the populace of this part of Mississippi. My family mourns death much as they celebrate life—right out loud. They cry, they laugh, they hug, and they eat. It has been accurately said that food is the love language of the South.

"Remember when Cletus and Joseph took Helen up on the barn roof when she was a baby and gave her chewing tobacco?" asks

1

Aunt Tiny, who apparently has given up on making Aunt Helen behave with decorum.

"Probably what made me go blind," adds Helen, and they are off on another round of family stories.

The laughter feels good and right, but it doesn't cushion the hard, cold fact that Daddy is gone. I am an orphan, *I think.* A forty-four-year-old orphan.

I look around and am startled when I catch sight of myself in the gilt-framed mirror on the far side of the room. I don't feel like the woman I see there. She is poised and fashionable, though rather strained. I look away and see Uncle Cletus checking a spray of peonies for hidden microphones in case the government or some alien civilization has tracked him down. I smile, remembering the many times I aided and abetted Cletus in his on-going war against all those who are "out to get him." That's better. I recognize this Evangeline Tanner; the one in the mirror is a stranger to me today.

After the graveside service, we all go back to the house for lunch. It's my house now, but it has been home as well to Aunt Lavinia, Uncle Calvin, and Uncle Cletus since my mother died. Aunt Lavinia felt it was her Christian duty to stay and help Daddy raise me, so she and Uncle Calvin moved out of their house in Mount Olive and in with us. Uncle Cletus apparently just never got around to leaving, and the five of us lived in the big blue house in Collins until I grew up and left them to carry on without me years ago.

When all the friends, neighbors, and family—except Aunt Helen— are gone, it is midafternoon and I go upstairs to change clothes and lie down. When I hang my black skirt and jacket in the closet

2

of my old bedroom, I see, pushed into the corner of the long, deep shelf, the faded and ragged forty-ounce Whitman Sampler candy box in which for years I put mementos of events as far ranging as my second-grade Christmas program to Mama's funeral. I pull it down and place it in the middle of the bed, remembering that day long ago when it came into my possession.

THE PROPOSAL

"Shift."

Whump! I fell out of the sagging double bed seconds after the mumbled command. Rubbing my head, I looked up into the untroubled eyes of my cousin, Linda Sue. "I said, 'shift,'" she said.

Shift meant turn over, but I was as yet unused to sleeping in a bed with two or three other girls, and ignorant of the lingo. At home, it was just me and Mama and Daddy, and I had a bed to myself where I could turn right over whenever I wanted to. Uncle Brantley and Aunt Tiny just had a two-bedroom house, so my four cousins had to share a bed, and in order for one to turn over, all had to turn. Well, technically, the oldest, Caroline, had a little single bed up against the wall, but she refused to sleep in it ever since Linda Sue hid the rubber snake under the covers. But it was hers, and nobody else dared to sleep in it. Not even Linda Sue. Tonight, since we were visiting, her mama made Caroline sleep there and put me in the big bed. The youngest two of us got the outsides.

That meant that the youngest got short shrift when it came to back scratching. Before we fell asleep, everybody scratched the back of the person on their left and then, "Shift," and everybody turned over and scratched the back on their right. Well, that meant me and Abbie, she was six, only got our backs scratched every other turn. It didn't seem fair, but it was more than I got at home, so I figured I shouldn't complain.

I got up rubbing my behind where it had hit the wood planks. It was summer, so my shortie pajamas didn't provide much padding. I climbed back in bed and turned my head as far as I could to talk to Linda Sue behind me.

"Want to know a secret?" I whispered.

"If you tell me, it won't be a secret." Linda Sue could be kind of a smart aleck sometimes.

I turned my head forward and plumped my pillow and closed my eyes.

"Well?" she asked after a few minutes.

I made a big deal out of yawning and said as sleepily as I could manage, "Well, what?"

"What's the secret?"

"If I tell you, it won't be a secret."

"Come on, tell." Linda Sue shoved closer and I felt myself moving toward the edge of the bed again.

"Cut it out."

"Tell."

"It's not really a secret, I don't guess. Just something I heard," I said airily.

Linda Sue was having none of it. "About what?" she asked, starting to nudge me again.

"About . . . Caroline's marriage proposal."

"Whaaaa?" gasped Linda Sue. "What are you talking about? Do you mean Alton?"

I yawned and stretched as much as it was possible to on my little dab of mattress to keep the suspense up. "Come on, give," she demanded.

"Would you two girls shut up?" Caroline mumbled sleepily from the other bed.

I froze and waited a minute for Caroline to start breathing deep again, then slipped out of bed and pulled on Linda Sue's arm to get her to follow me. We tiptoed down the hall to the kitchen and closed the door.

"Come on, tell," she said, opening the refrigerator door so she could see my face.

"Well, maybe I shouldn't. I'm not supposed to know," I said and looked toward the ceiling like I was seeking guidance from the Lord.

Linda Sue pinched a blue place on my arm and repeated, "Tell."

"Okay, okay, you don't have to get violent." I scooted closer to the refrigerator and told.

"When I got back from the store today, I heard Alton talking to Uncle Brantley out in the garage. He asked for 'Miss Caroline's hand,'" I said, doing a fair impression of Alton's long, deep drawl. We started giggling, but then remembered we weren't supposed to be up in the middle of the night telling secrets in the refrigerator and got serious again. "Your daddy said it was fine by him and Alton started pumping Uncle Brantley's hand up and down and thanking him until Uncle Brantley said, 'By God, man, you're gone break my arm.' Then Alton said he was gonna come over here today and ask her before he got too scared to. Uncle Brantley told him y'all were going to the river about three and Alton said he'd be here directly after lunch. No later than 1:30, he said."

"Well, poor old Alton. I hope he knows what he's doing," said Linda Sue.

"I plan on watching it," I said.

"How?"

"Well, a long time ago when we were playing hide and seek, I found this little knot hole in the living room paneling. If you get in the hall closet, you can see and hear everything going on in there. I've never seen a proposal before, and you know I plan to be a writer or an artist and I need to know about these things."

"Hmmph," Linda Sue snorted and then she kind of shivered. I thought maybe it was because I had encouraged her to think about the deep, romantic things in life, but then she said the ham for tomorrow's dinner was poking into her backside and was about to freeze her to death. "You watch if you want to," she said. "I'm supposed to go to Donna Johnson's after lunch, but you can tell me about it when I get back. Or maybe you can draw it for me." She kind of sneered when she said that, and for a minute I wondered why I had always thought of her as my favorite cousin. Just like everybody else, she didn't believe I would ever be anything but a housewife.

We went back to bed, but I didn't sleep real good. I didn't want to miss a "shift" and end up on the floor again. The next morning I hung around Caroline and tried to find out if she knew Alton's intentions. She was real crabby, calling me a nosy pest, so I figured she did know and was nervous about becoming a fiancée. That's what they call engaged women. I learned that when Edna Ross got engaged last year. Daddy said it should be called the financee, in her case, and poor old Joey Hargruder is the financer.

Caroline was as closed mouthed as a snapping turtle clamped down on a stick, so I gave up and went looking for crawdads with Linda Sue until lunch. Neither me nor Caroline ate much of the turnip greens and cornbread Aunt Tiny cooked. I figured Caroline was too excited to eat, but I just hate turnip greens. They're right up there with liver on the "Do Not Eat" list. Why would anybody want to eat something's liver? And turnip greens? Just taste them.

I offered to help with the dishes and Daddy gave me a little pat on the head like he was proud of me for being so grown up. I felt a little guilty about operating under false pretenses, because the real reason I did it was I wanted to have an excuse to be close to the hall closet come 1:20 or so. But I wasn't guilty enough to change my mind. I drug around real slow, and then told Aunt Tiny I'd finish up so she could rest. She eyed me like I was a horn worm on a tomato plant for a minute and I thought I'd overplayed my hand, but then she went on out to the front porch swing with a glass of sweet tea.

I finished up the rest of that kitchen faster than the Tasmanian Devil on the Bugs Bunny cartoon and slipped into the hall closet with my own glass of tea at 1:25, just seconds before Alton came walking up the front steps. Apparently Caroline didn't have any idea that this was her big day after all, because when Aunt Tiny let Alton in and yelled to Caroline that he was here, I heard Caroline say, "Darn it," which in Mama's opinion was a by-word and was almost as bad as a swear word. But since Mama wasn't there to hear it, nobody did anything about it and after about ten minutes Caroline finally showed up in the living room. I leaned closer to the knot hole, thinking I'd have to open it up a little more for a better view, and wishing I'd thought to bring in a stool or something to sit on. I had to hunch over under the shelf and lean forward to see.

I just got in position when I heard something scratching at the door. For a minute I thought I was found out, then I heard mewing. Linda Sue's black-and-white cat, Little Joe, was trying to get his paw under the door. (Linda Sue loved the TV Western *Bonanza*, and Little Joe Cartwright in particular.) I opened the door and tried to shoo the cat away, but that just got him yowling like I had dunked him in ice water, so I opened the door enough he could see me and that shut him up.

"What you doin' here today, Alton?" Caroline was asking real grumpy like when I got back to the knot hole. "I was getting ready to go to the river."

Alton kind of slumped over, I guess because he was so tall Caroline had to arch her neck backwards to look straight at him. He kind of screwed his face up—which wasn't a good idea, considering he already looked a whole lot like Freddy Baker's three-legged wiener dog—then cleared his throat. He leaned toward Caroline, then leaned back away, then cleared his throat again. "What IS it, Alton?" Caroline said, finally plopping down on the green vinyl couch right under the front window. Alton followed her over and stood beside the couch. They were directly across from the peep hole I had made in the hall closet through that paneling knot. It was like wiggling the rabbit ears on the television. I could see perfect.

"Uh," Alton said. "Ah, Miss Caroline, there's something I want to say."

"Speak on, Alton." Caroline was studying a spot on the arm of the couch. She wet her finger with spit and rubbed the vinyl, while Alton shifted from one foot to the other.

"Ah, it's more like there's something I want to ask you."

Caroline sat up straight, dirt spot forgotten, and stared at Alton. I think the picture was coming in clearer for her, too.

"What, Alton? What do you want to ask?"

"Go for it, Alton," I whispered and took a sip of tea. The ice rattled so loud I thought sure they'd come dragging me out of that closet any minute. I stood stock still until I couldn't hold onto that cold glass any more. But Alton and Caroline were apparently deaf, so I set the glass down on the shelf over my head.

Alton took a deep breath then got down on one knee beside the couch. He stayed that way a minute, like he was as frozen as my right hand, then he reached out, kinda jerky like, and grabbed her hand. The same one she had spit on.

"Miss Caroline," he finally began, "we've been stepping out together for some time now and I think you know how I feel about you."

"No, Alton. How do you feel?" Caroline asked. She wasn't going to make this easy, it seemed.

"Well, I think you're a fine girl." No response. "And I think you're a good cook." Caroline was quiet. "You keep a good house," Alton tried then. Caroline began to stare at him, stone faced and silent. She didn't even blink that I could see. Of course, I was way across the room and looking through a knot hole.

Alton turned beet red and I think the eye on the side I could see started twitching. It was hard to tell from that distance, but I know it does that sometimes when he gets nervous. Like that time

10

Caroline threw the milk shake he brought her right in the middle of his shirt because he hadn't ironed the shirt before he came over. Caroline could be like that.

My back was beginning to ache and I straightened up before I thought and smacked right into the shelf, knocking my tea over and making a goose egg the size of Texas on my head. I knew there was no way they didn't hear that, so I jumped out of the closet and stepped right on Little Joe's tail, setting him squalling like he was killed. I had just picked him up when Caroline and Alton came around the corner.

"What in tarnation is going on?" Caroline asked.

If I had any creative genes, now was the time for them to manifest.

"I, uh, I came to get a drink of water and Little Joe must have gotten locked in the hall closet," I said. *Not bad.* "I heard a racket in there and opened the door and there he was. Poor baby. He must have been so scared."

I put my face down in Joe's fur and looked out of the corner of my eye at Caroline. They turned and went back out. *Yes.*

I made a point of leaving the kitchen noisily, put Joe outside, then quietly made my way back to the closet. I was just in time to hear Alton say, "You're the purtiest girl in three counties and I want to marry you and I want you to be my wife and cook for me and keep my house."

Caroline kept staring at him a few minutes like she was waiting for more, then she looked at her left hand, then back up at him, then cocked her head to one side like she was considering. Then she said, "Isn't there something more you'd like to do? To give me?" All the while she was holding her hand out like she wanted him to kiss it. Alton looked at it for a minute, then he jumped up and nearly hit the living room light fixture. Looking as excited and relieved as a coon dog that's just been let out of his truck crate, Alton reached behind the couch and grabbed a huge box wrapped in brown grocery-bag paper, dumped it in her lap,

11

and said, "I have brung you a token of my affections." Then he dropped back down on his knee, while Caroline stared at the box.

Finally, he reached over and tore off the paper, revealing a big yellow box. "I love you, Miss Caroline, and I'm asking for yore hand in marriage." Caroline picked up the box, then stood up, looking like she had tasted something nastier than turnip greens or liver.

"Candy?" she yelled. "Candy? You don't propose to a girl with a box of candy!"

Shoot. Even I knew that, and I had never been proposed to even once.

"I thought you liked candy, Miss Caroline. Especially these Whitman Samplers, and this one's the biggest I ever seen." Alton was even redder, if you can imagine it, almost purple. He was about to get up, but fell back on his knee when Caroline smacked him on the head with the candy box.

"Candy . . . is not . . . an . . . engagement ring, . . .Alton," she ground out, then flounced out of the room. I had heard people talk about flouncing, but I had never really seen it before. When she got to the bedroom door, she turned and heaved that candy box back down the hall. I could hear it hit the wall and bounce off.

Alton stood up slowly, rubbing the side of his head, and mumbled, "I sure thought she'd like that Whitman Sampler." He opened the front screen and stepped out, muttering, "It's the biggest one I ever seen."

I came out of the closet real slow to make sure nobody saw me, then picked up the Whitman candy box. "Hey," I yelled, like I didn't know where anybody was. "There's a big old box of candy in the floor. What should I do with it?"

Caroline slammed the door open, stared at me and the candy and said, "Throw it in the garbage. I never want to see a Whitman's Sampler again," then slammed the door shut.

"Done," I said, then I skedaddled with the candy before she could change her mind. I headed over to Donna Johnson's to tell her and Linda Sue all about the proposal.

Caroline finally did marry Alton, but first he had to buy her a diamond ring. And keep his shirts ironed.

I was terribly disappointed in the proposal, as my sense of romance was as finely honed as my cousin Denver's filet knife. But my belief in handkerchief-clutching, heart-throbbing romance, complete with heaving bosoms, was justified a few years later. To commemorate the event, I had kept a piece of a menu from the Pancake Platter.

FARMING AT
THE PANCAKE PLATTER

My cousin Otis married Beverly Ann Burkhalter last month. They eloped. I think that's the most romantic thing I ever heard of. I want to elope, too. But, first, I have to have a boyfriend. Daddy says I can't date until I'm seventeen, but neither could Beverly Ann and that didn't stop her. She's fifteen and two grades ahead of me. We were in gym class in junior high school, but now she goes to Collins High School.

Beverly Ann and Otis have been boyfriend/girlfriend since fifth grade. I fell in love with Scott Simpson in first grade and thought I'd marry him one day. But in fifth grade, he asked Carla Klingman to be his Valentine and that was the end of that. I liked Armstrong Pitts a little bit after that, but that was doomed.

The first week in seventh grade, I started liking a really cute boy named Steve Kennedy, but he didn't know I was alive. I sat right behind him in physical science and he was the sunshine that got my chlorophyll all stirred up. But he was a town kid and thought I was a hick, I guess. Anyway he flirted with Amy Brown, the short, cute cheerleader whose daddy owned the drug store. Amy always had beauty shop haircuts and store-bought clothes, while I had Aunt Lavinia. Aunt Lavinia worked really hard sewing dresses and skirts for me and I appreciated it, but she seemed to think I'd always be ten years old. She made these flouncy-skirted things with sashes in the back. Worse yet, last summer she put one of those Toni permanent waves in my hair.

15

She said I'd look like a movie star. And I sure did—like Shirley Temple. No wonder Steve never looked my way.

Anyway, like I said, I'd really like to elope sometime. Either that or suffer unrequited love like poor Heathcliff in *Wuthering Heights*. I really wasn't supposed to read that book, but Miss Newcastle took Miss Funderburke's place at the library last June and ever since then I can check out most anything I want to.

I kind of like J.R. Barber in my English class because he's dark and mysterious and nobody knows if his last name is really Barber or Berringer, and he has a deep voice like a grown man, even though he is a little bit short. But wiry. I might elope with him when I'm a little older. Maybe next year.

Otis's parents are mad as all get out about Otis and Beverly Ann, but I don't see why. I heard Uncle Wilson tell Daddy that Otis's life is over. Otis is ruined, he said. I've never had a ruined cousin before, so I decided to make it my business to find out more about it. Daddy told Uncle Wilson to calm down, that Otis wasn't the first one in our neck of the woods to have a shotgun wedding. I wonder why they call it that. Neck of the woods. I'd say, "our region of the country," but then somebody would tell me I was being high falutin'. But I'm not. I just think it makes better sense to say what you mean. But a shotgun wedding. I wonder how they got one of those. The way Beverly Ann told it to all the girls in gym class, according to Mary Beth McClendon's big sister, Amy, was that they just went to Alabama and got a judge to marry them right there in the courthouse. Old Mr. Barton, who lived behind the library in Mount Olive, had a twenty-one-gun salute at his funeral because he fought in the World War. I never can remember which one, but he was really old, so maybe the first one. I can't imagine a judge letting anybody do that at a marriage ceremony in the courthouse, though. It's pretty dramatic, but not very romantic. Daddy noticed me in the hall right after he said that and went outside to talk and I didn't dare follow him, so I had to gather my intelligence somewhere else. That's what I like to call getting information. If I was a boy, I'd join the FBI or the CIA, but I don't guess women are allowed. I told Cletus I'm training for the FBI just to see his reaction. He locks his room now and won't look at me at the table, and I feel kind of bad for saying it. I don't think Mama would think I was being very kind.

Gathering intelligence from Daddy and Uncle Wilson was a dead-end after that one conversation, but the women in Aunt Lavinia's sewing circle were too busy gossiping to notice I was listening, so I heard a lot from them. It didn't clear things up much, though. Aunt Lavinia told Mrs. Monahan that Beverly Ann's mother locked her in her room for a week, and Mrs. Monahan said it didn't do any good to lock the barn after the cow got out. That didn't make a lot of sense to start talking about farming right in the middle of a conversation about Otis and Beverly Ann, but Mrs. Monahan may have senile dementia since she's way over fifty. Then Mrs. Carmichael said they weren't the first young couple to put the cart before the horse, so I figured Otis and Beverly Ann are going to be farmers, but aren't very good at it. Particularly after Mary Beth McClendon's mother said they got what was coming to them. "You don't spend your Saturday nights sowing wild oats," she said, 'then go to church on Sunday morning and pray for crop failure." The ladies all started laughing and I did too, but then they noticed me and sent me outside.

I went to ask Daddy where Otis and Beverly Ann were going to have their farm, but just as I walked out I heard Uncle Wilson say that Otis was dropping out of school and had gotten a job at the Pancake Platter in Collins. He'd be working as a busboy.

"A busboy," Uncle Wilson said. "He could have been a doctor. A lawyer. A senator."

Now, I think that was a little optimistic, but still, a busboy might be on the low end of the opportunity spectrum, even for Otis. I think he'd be better off to get the farm on the right track.

"Now, Wilson," Daddy said. "He'll be alright. You have to admire the boy. He did the right thing and he's being responsible."

Knowing Daddy approved of eloping made me feel better about my idea of maybe running away with J.R. next year. If I could get him to be my boyfriend. Of course, I didn't want to quit school or have J.R. quit either. Maybe I better go with the unrequited love, at least until I graduate high school. That's just about as romantic. I could sit in my room and write sad poetry and be famous after I die.

While I was thinking about that, Scott and Zelda, my Australian Shepherds, came around the corner with their puppies, and I got caught up playing with them and didn't hear what Uncle Wilson said. I kept thinking about it all, though. I just didn't see how Otis would have time to learn how to be a better farmer if he was working all the time at the Pancake Platter. Beverly Ann might have to run the farm all by herself, but according to what the sewing circle ladies said, she didn't seem to have any better idea how to do it than Otis did.

After supper, I told Daddy I was going to save my allowance and buy a book on farming to give to Otis and Beverly Ann as a wedding present. He looked at me funny and asked, "Why a book on farming?"

"So Otis can quit the Pancake Platter and help Beverly Ann make a go of the farm."

"What farm? They're living with the Burkhalters until after the . . . until they get on their feet," Daddy said.

"Well, Aunt Lavinia and her sewing ladies were talking today about how bad Otis and Beverly Ann are at farming," I said. "Mrs. Carmichael said they don't even know how to hitch up a horse. Although I imagine they'll get a tractor, and Otis already has a truck, so I don't see why they even need a horse and cart."

Daddy screwed up his face like I had grown another eyebrow and asked what in tarnation I was talking about. I told him what the ladies had said and how I thought farming would be a better life than working at a restaurant, so I was gonna get them that book.

Daddy turned red, then purple, then kind of gray, so I asked him if he needed an aspirin or something. He said no, what he needed was my mama, so I figured all this talk about marrying was making him miss her again.

"Vangie," he said, and I didn't know why he said it that way, like each letter weighed more than his tongue could hold. "I'm afraid it's time you and me had a little talk." The last time I heard those words in that particular way was when I was eleven and Mama gave me "The Talk."

Sure enough, it was related, and I was about purple, too, before Daddy finished explaining to me that the wild oats Otis and Beverly Ann had sown had very little in common with the corn fields. That decided it for me, though. I'm going to get started on the sad poetry, just as soon as I can get my heart broken by J.R.

J.R. didn't break my heart, but he did make me mad enough to tie his picture to a stick of wood and burn it in the backyard when I caught him kissing Debbie Messinger in the closet by the band hall after school. He apparently forgot he was supposed to meet me there and when I opened the door, there they were.

I remember storming out of the school, marching straight home and getting the kitchen matches. I danced around that little "stake" with his picture on it, whooping like I imagined would make my Native American ancestors proud. I may have been a tad dramatic as a youth.

After traveling this bit of memory lane, I go downstairs for a glass of sweet tea, then return to my room and the Whitman candy box. Sampler is an appropriate name for it still, but instead of chocolates, it now holds a varied assortment of time fragments from my years growing up in this house.

I take a sip of the tea, very sweet and almost jet black. Mama used to say Aunt Lavinia made syrup, not tea, but I have always liked it. Settling back on the pillows propped on the headboard, I rummage in the box of memories. When I pull out the Mogen David label, I am bombarded with a variety of memories, but only the first one makes me laugh, so I concentrate on it.

STRONG DRINK

On the way to Miss Rachel Katz's house, I had to pass the shame of Covington County. Our town, Collins, was a God-fearing little community near the Covington and Smith county lines. Covington was a dry county. I used to think it didn't rain there as much as it did in Forrest County, but I found out that wasn't what a dry county meant. I found that out at the same time I found out what the shame of Covington County was. Or, rather, who.

Edgar and Alva Atmore lived on Elm Street, three doors down from Miss Rachel. I usually went to Miss Rachel's on Saturday afternoons and I never saw or heard anybody at the Atmores' house. Until one Friday night when I went to have what Miss Rachel called the Shabbat meal. Shabbat was apparently the Sabbath in her country.

As I was passing their house, the front door banged open and out rolled two fat, old, nearly naked people, arms and legs flailing. They rolled right down the front steps into the yard, screaming, punching, slapping, and Lord knows what all else. I stopped dead still when I heard Alva Atmore yell, "You SOB (I'm not allowed to repeat what she really said), you cut my leg."

"Well, you threw hot pork chops in my face." Edgar punched Alva in the stomach.

She raked her nails down his face. "You said they tasted like slop, so I threw them to the closest hog, you sorry bastard."

I don't think I'm supposed to repeat that one either, but I don't know any other way to say it.

I saw blood running down Alva's leg when they rolled closer to me. I wanted to run, but I couldn't seem to make my legs move. I couldn't even make my eyes blink. The closest I'd ever come to seeing violence was when my cousin Davey and me put a cherry bomb in Old Mr. McEntyre's mailbox and he surprised us and came outside right as it blew. Other than that it was just gunfights on *Bonanza*, but that wasn't real.

But here it was. Violence. Right under my very eyes. I tried to think what I should do and then I heard a siren. The police chief, Barry Cole, pulled up to the curb, jumped out, and tried to pull the Atmores off each other. Alva landed a good punch to Chief Cole's left eye before he got them separated.

I managed to move backward a little way under an oak tree— Elm Street was full of big old oaks—and nobody even seemed to notice I was there. The neighbors were all standing in their yards watching Edgar and Alva beating the tar out of each other.

"Edgar, Alva, this time you're going to jail," the chief said.

"He should go to jail, the murdering SOB," Alva yelled.

"I didn't do nothin'. I just tried to protect myself." Edgar was slapping at the air in Alva's direction. "You tried to burn my face off, you fat witch."

Only he didn't say witch, but I know not to use that word for sure. Because I did once.

"Look here, Chief." Alva held out her bare leg. All she had on was a ripped nylon slip. Blood ran from a deep gash in her right calf. "He tried to kill me."

"Aww. I just bit her leg," Edgar protested.

Just then, Sam Carter, the other Collins police officer, drove up and got out. "At it again?" he said. "First of the month, just like clockwork."

"Let's put these two in the car, Sam," Chief Cole said. "On second thought, better put one in my car and one in yours."

"What about my leg?" Alva yelled. "If I die, I'll sue you bastards."

"We'll take you by the hospital, Alva, get you stitched up," Officer Carter said.

"She ain't hurt," Edgar said. "I just bit her leg a little after she hit me with a bottle then tried to stab me with it when it broke."

"You hit me with a plate."

"You threw the plate at me first and burned my face all up with them pork chops."

"Both of you shut up and get in the car," Chief Cole said, half dragging Edgar over to the patrol car. Edgar had on an undershirt and torn boxer shorts.

Officer Carter shoved Alva over to the chief's car and pushed her into the back seat. It wasn't easy; she was a lot bigger than him and was fighting and swinging all the way. After getting the Atmores locked into the cars, the two officers went into the house and came back out a few minutes later with a box of empty bottles and a hatchet with drying blood on the blade.

"They sure tore that place up," Officer Carter was saying.

"They always do," said Chief Cole. "I'll be glad when they finish each other off and we don't have to come out here every blame month."

"At least they can't afford to go to Hattiesburg to get booze until they get their checks," Officer Carter said. "It gives us some sort of break."

"Blamed sots." The chief got in his car. As the door opened, I heard Alva still going on about her leg, her murdering SOB of a husband, and how she was suing the police department, the City of Collins, and maybe all of Covington County.

As both cars drove away, I walked on to Miss Rachel's. My legs were all trembly and I couldn't forget Mrs. Atmore's leg with the blood running down. What would make people act like that?

When I asked Miss Rachel that very question, she said it was the alcohol, but wouldn't say another word about it. She just poured her wine and we sat down to supper.

When I got home, I told Mama and Daddy what happened. Daddy tried not to laugh when I told how Edgar kept saying he just bit Alva's leg, even while the police stood there with a bloody hatchet. Mama said, "Wine is a mocker and strong drink is raging." She fixed me with a look like I'd been in on the carryings on with the Atmores and added, "That, Evangeline, is exactly why our church covenant says we will abstain from the sale and use of alcohol."

Apparently, Edgar and Alva weren't members of a missionary Baptist church. "Daddy," I said, "Why do the Atmores act all crazy like that? Miss Rachel said it was the alcohol, and Mama said strong drink is raging, but Miss Rachel drinks wine and she's never tried to hatchet my leg or anything." I started to tell him that Linda DeBenedetto's parents drank wine, too, and Mr. DeBenedetto drank something called Scotch, but then I thought I might get in trouble for hanging around with Catholics, so I kept that to myself. Daddy explained that Edgar and Alva were alcoholics (apparently sot is another name for alcoholic) and when they got what he called all liquored up, they always fought. "They just went at it a little harder this time," he said. "They're two peaceable people when they aren't drunk."

Now that was something to think about. I didn't want to be a sot and hatchet people's legs, but I had always thought the dark purplish wine in the fancy glasses was really pretty. Miss Rachel always had wine at her Shabbat meal. She said it was Kosher, but I thought kosher was pickles. I didn't want to seem ignorant, so I didn't ask. It was my intention to serve wine to my guests when I grew up and was an artist or a writer or an FBI agent. I had read in books where the people in Italy always drank wine in crystal goblets and the people in Germany drank ale and beer in fancy glasses called tankards and steins. It never seemed to cause any problems. Well, there was Hitler, so maybe beer was a mistake. I decided to stick to wine and maybe Scotch. Miss Rachel and the DeBenedettos were never mean and crazy.

I guess I better find out if there are any branches of Baptists that don't have to sign a covenant, so I can have goblets and drink wine and still go to heaven. I know one thing, I'll never ask Mama over to dinner, and I'll never leave any sharp knives laying around—just in case.

I pick up the tea, wishing it was, indeed, a glass of wine, but a pinot noir, not Mogen David. I take a drink of the tea, and the amber liquid reminds me of the time I tried Scotch. I had spent the night with Linda DeBenedetto. Her parents had gone to mass and left us to ourselves. Linda swiped a bottle of Chivas Regal from the den and brought it up to her bedroom, along with two water glasses. The Scotch was an inviting caramel color and the word Scotch made me think of my favorite Lifesavers candy flavor, butterscotch. My mouth watered at the thought, I recall. I had slugged down a good bit before my taste buds got wind of what I was doing, but my stomach wasted no time in evicting the offending substance. I still can't smell hard liquor without gagging.

I put the Mogen David label back, not ready to deal with the other memories it evokes, and smile when I pull out a Chiquita Banana sticker. It always made me think of the Bonanno crime family, which was my coded reminder for the Pitts brothers. I was quite big on codes.

THE PITTS

Buddy Ray Pitts named his twin boys Harold and Armstrong. You know he knew what was gonna happen. And sure enough. By the time they hit third grade, Harry and Arm Pitts were the toughest boys in Collins Elementary. I don't think Mr. Pitts did it to make his boys tough; he just thought it'd be a hoot. "Arm Pitts," he'd yell out the trailer door, then bust out laughing like a mad man. Armstrong never dared give his father any grief, but at school, anybody that giggled about Harry Pitts or Arm Pitts would likely be giggling through a few fewer teeth.

I'm friends with them, but I always make sure to use their whole names. I don't believe in violence, especially when I'm on the receiving end. I'm not allowed to go to their house because they live in a trailer down near the dump and their mama ran off when the twins were two weeks old. Maybe because of their names. Maybe she couldn't face spending the rest of her life with Harry Arm Pitts. It's pretty funny. But not if you were their mama, I guess. Or them.

Anyway, they come to my house a lot and we catch crawdads by the creek and climb the big oak in our front yard. I like to take a book up there and read, but Harold and Armstrong aren't big on books. Sometimes, we walk in the woods with my dogs, and their hounds, Lolly and Pop. That name thing must run in the blood. Once I made a joke, saying if they'd had a sister, they could have named her Nasturtium and called her Nasty Pitts, but they bristled up like porcupines so fast, I let that go. We talked about all kinds of other things, though, and we've stayed friends right up through

27

sixth grade. They'll go to the county junior high, though, and I'll be in Collins, so I don't know what will happen then.

I have to admit, I've always been a little sweet on Armstrong, but I'd never let on to my other friends. Who wants to tell anybody that their first kiss was with Arm Pitts? It made me think a lot about what I'd name my children if I ever had any. And I guess I will because Mama said that was what the Good Lord made women for, to raise a family. According to Uncle Calvin, Shakespeare said a rose by any other name would smell as sweet, but try telling that to a boy named Harry Pitts.

"Harold," I said the other day when we were making clover chains in the back yard, "what are you gonna do when you grow up?"

"I'm 'on be rich."

"How you gone do that, Harry?" asked Armstrong, the only person in Covington County besides Buddy Ray that would have dared use the nick name.

"I'm 'on go into bidness." Now we've had the same teachers since Miss Brooker in first grade, but those boys talk trailer like their daddy. My Mama would skin me alive if I ever said "bidness."

"What kind of business, Harold?" I asked.

"Not moonshine," he said. "Something respectable, but still with lots of money and power, like those banana people in New York."

"I'm 'on go to school and make a lawyer," said Armstrong. "And defend rich people and be rich, too."

"I think Harry Pitts Bonanno is going to need a lawyer," I thought, but I didn't say it out loud. I didn't want the boys to choke me with my own clover chain.

"Daddy," I said later that night. "Do you think people really get to decide what they want to be? Or do they just kind of get caught up in what their families have always been? Or what they're expected to be?"

Daddy was real quiet for a while, just staring at the television in the corner, even though it wasn't turned on. "Well, take me," he finally said. "My people expected me to make a preacher like my father and grandfather before me." Mama was mending a rip in one of my blouses and she jabbed herself in the hand and kind of half squealed, half snorted. Daddy gave her a mean look and that's not like Daddy. Why in the world would he get mad at Mama for stabbing her hand with a needle?

"But I didn't want that life," Daddy continued a little louder, still glaring at Mama. "I left home before I was grown to ease the burden on Ma. Pa was gone a lot preaching the Word. We wouldn't hear from him for weeks or months and it was all on Ma to provide for us. I did some farmin', and some mechanicin' and when I could make 'em believe I was eighteen, I joined the Army. When I got out, I met your mama and we got married. With a glance in Mama's direction, he added almost under his breath, "Met on Sunday and got married on Friday. How 'bout that?" Before I could comment, he went on, "Then I had to learn a trade."

Mama left the room, then, and I thought I heard her snort again and say, "Preacher," under her breath, but that didn't make a lot of sense. Her own daddy was a preacher and she had all kinds of respect for him. She even made me wear dresses and put away the dominoes when he came to visit.

"I got on with Larry Jones Plumbing," Daddy continued, "and Larry taught me to be a plumber. So, I guess I made a choice. I reckon everybody can choose if they want to."

I went up to my room and thought about what Daddy said, but I guess that really only applies to boys. Mama always tells me I need to come down out of the tree and learn about cooking and sewing and house cleaning, so I'll make a good wife when the time comes. She says I need to study Proverbs 31, so I can be a virtuous woman whose price is far above rubies. I read it one day in Mrs. Katz's Bible, but her copy's defective. It's missing the whole second half, but it did have Proverbs. Just to be sure, though, I went home and looked it up in my King James that has my name written in gold right on the front. It sounds to me like all a wife does is work, spinning and making quilts and such, while her husband gets to sit around at the city gates and be praised. I guess that's what I've got to look forward to.

Mama seems happy with the arrangement, but sometimes I think about what would happen if I decided not to get married. I could have a career. All my teachers have been women and they were all married, except for Miss Brooker, but they had careers. Or what if I ran away and became a movie star, or an artist? I could be a writer like Eudora Welty or Flannery O'Connor. I read some of their stuff in the library, but Mrs. Funderburke made me go back to the juvenile section. The only thing good in the juvenile section are the blue biographies and I've already read all them.

I carry around a notebook all the time and draw the comic strip characters from the Sunday paper. I can draw pretty good. Maybe I can be a real artist and live in New York. I can write, too. Nobody knew it, but I wrote a story when I was in fourth grade. I wanted to get it published, but I didn't know where to send it, so it's still in a box under my bed.

I don't want to disappoint Mama, but I sure don't want to spend the rest of my life cooking, sewing, canning vegetables, and cleaning like a mad woman on Saturdays. I know one thing for sure and certain. If I do have to marry somebody, it won't be anybody like Buddy Ray Pitts. If he sits around the city gates, it's because he's too drunk to walk back to the trailer.

Buddy Ray Pitts wasn't the only deterrent to the idea of marriage. There were also my alternating dreams of being a rich and famous actress, a rich and famous author, and a Bohemian artist—a rich and famous one, of course.

Then came the day when I ate of the tree of the knowledge of good and evil.

THE WORLD BOOK

I believe the course of my whole life was set in the spring of 1960. That was when a door-to-door salesman came through town and talked my mama into buying the entire set of *World Book Encyclopedia*—with an annual update for five years.

I had learned to read before I was five, but even so I'm pretty sure I just looked at the pictures for a while. I mean, this was an encyclopedia after all and was probably a bit much for a six-year-old to take in. It wasn't long, though, before I was looking up stuff to beat the band.

Anytime I saw a new word or heard something interesting on the radio, or the TV after we finally got one, I went straight to the *World Book*. The set was displayed on a long wooden shelf in our living room like other people display fine china. I'd take the C out to look up Chinchilla and end up learning about China and even chocolate. Did you know that the swirls on top of the candies in a box of chocolates tell you what kind it is? If my cousin Caroline knew that, she wouldn't have a bite gone out of every piece in the box. She could go straight for the coconut creams.

It was the *World Book* that taught me that the horse Roy Rogers rode was a Golden Palomino. It was right there in full color in the middle of the Hs. Dale Evans rode a buttermilk buckskin. The array of horseflesh displayed in the two-page layout of breeds is probably what sparked my life-long admiration of *equus caballus*.

And horses were just the tip of that educational iceberg. I learned that our cat, Haley Mills, was most likely a domestic shorthair, and Jonathon Bing, my first dog, was at least part feist. His name was Blackie at first, because Daddy named him, but I changed it to Jonathon Bing when I was in third grade. Everybody I met wanted to buy that dog for a squirrel dog. But I wasn't about to part with Jonathon Bing.

My mama got annoyed with me sometimes because I would try to teach her about stuff. Sometimes she did things way different than the *World Book* said was best, and when I pointed out a better way, she'd get all irritated. Like when Haley had kittens. I tried to tell Mama that we should give her egg yolk and cod liver oil to help her make milk to feed the babies, but Mama said all she cared about was keeping the frazzlin fleas out of the frazzlin stuffed animals in the closet Haley chose to give birth in. The *World Book* and I were asked to vacate the premises. That's kind of a euphemism. What she really said was, "Take that frazzlin book and go outside while I still have hair left in my head." I learned about euphemisms in the Merriam Webster, not the *World Book*.

Sometimes, learning about things in the *World Book* isn't really the best way to go about it. A little information can be as bad as—or worse than—no information at all if you don't understand it. Like I said, with the *World Book*, I'd go to look up something and then I'd see something else that caught my interest and read about that, too. There was the time I woke up in the night with a stomach ache. I had had a stomach ache before, but this was different. I was throwing up, too. So I did what I figured was best. I got out the *World Book* and, after some careful research, I diagnosed myself with a case of indigestion. I was about to go back to bed when the word "Indigo" caught my eye. I moved to the kitchen where the light was better so I could read about it, but then I started throwing up again. Right there on the kitchen floor. Before I could clean it up and go back to the bathroom, Mama got up to see what was going on. I tried to tell her I just had indigestion, but she took me to the hospital. Turns out I had acute appendicitis. If I hadn't gone to the kitchen and accidentally woke Mama up, the doctor said my appendix would have ruptured and killed me deader than a door nail. So, in a way, Indigo and the *World Book Encyclopedia* saved my life.

By the way, the *World Book* says a door nail is a large headed nail they used to put on doors back in olden days. I looked it up when I got out of the hospital. I guess you can't get much deader than that.

I've never been good at asking questions; I tend to try to find answers on my own. In the earliest years, I used the encyclopedia, but then I discovered the public library. When I found out about research libraries, it was practically Nirvana. I eventually came to realize that I often could have had a better answer in a fraction of the time just by asking someone who could be presumed to know. Still, the propensity to go it alone remains.

Aunt Lavinia climbs halfway up the stairs to ask if I want to come down for some supper. She will be seventy-five in a couple of months and the stairs are a trial for her. It is a supreme act of love for her to have navigated them for me. The thing I have just taken from the box closes my throat and stops in its tracks any appetite I might have had. I go to the door of my room, smile at her, and say, "No, thank you, Aunt Lavinia, I just want to be alone for a while." She nods and slowly makes her way back down, her shoulders stooped from age, grief, and bone weariness. "You should get some rest," I add gently, and she looks back and nods again.

I look in my hand at the little box, understanding that not everything can be researched, explained, expected, or easily coped with. Understanding also that I have to treasure the time I have with my family. The small innocuous match box vividly calls to mind the summer I turned thirteen.

THE SUMMER I TURNED THIRTEEN

"Evangeline," Mama called. I suspect she called me that way because Evangeline is my name. Other than that, I can think of no plausible reason for such an address. And I do try to think of reasons, because Mama may have an ulterior motive. I suspect I think that way because Mama usually does have some ulterior motive; in fact, Mama may just be an ulterior motive God has foisted on us here below.

"Evangeline, come see Uncle Cletus," she called a bit louder. Ah, ha! The motive. Uncle Cletus, while presumably harmless, is not someone I yearn daily to see. He is in the habit of wearing Kelly green slacks with red-and-blue-striped shirts, in combination with lizard skin boots and a straw Stetson. A Zippo adorned with a horse' head is never far from his hand. His mode of dress is the least of my objections, however; my greatest is his persistence in calling me "Girlie," and an unsavory aroma, semi-masked by bountiful splashes of Mennen Skin Bracer. Next in line, not really all that objectionable due to its potential for hours of interesting observation, is his paranoia. Cletus—sans Uncle, as I call in him my mind but never in the presence of Mama—regularly decides the neighbors, the local officials, and extraterrestrial beings have designs on his body and/or mind. His furniture stays gathered in a huddle in the middle of his living room floor to prevent enterprising members of the aforementioned categories from climbing through his windows and catching him unawares. Mama says we ought to have pity on a poor muddled creature and thank God above that we aren't in the same shape.

Daddy and I, however, think someone ought to have pity on the poor creatures that have to endure his skin bracer au naturale, namely me and Daddy. On this particular occasion, Cletus came to shed sweetness and light on our household for two weeks. What's more, additional members of the Tanner clan were expected to arrive within the next three days to share Daddy's birthday, Independence Day, and Homecoming at Crossroads Missionary Baptist Church. While Cletus is the indisputable worst, he is certainly not in a category by himself. He is flanked by Aunt Tiny, Aunt Lavinia, and Uncle Calvin. On the side of sanity are Grandpa MacRae, Uncle Tommy, and I guess that's about it, unless I count Mama, Daddy to some degree, and if I have the presumption to include myself, which I do. So, that makes six defenders of all that's within the bounds of normality and four who have absolutely no concept of reality.

A little insanity goes a long way, so that makes us just about even. This time Cletus had arrived earlier than the rest because the FBI was spying on his apartment, and he had to give them the slip and get over to our house before they figured out where the rest of the family lived. That accomplished, he brought in the army green AWOL bag that sheltered his most precious possessions—a spare pair of green slacks and a few copies of *Playboy*. I was given the task of accompanying him to his room and helping him move the bed away from the wall—the neighbors already knew where we lived—and generally getting him settled in.

"Hey, Uncle Cletus," I said, "I thought I saw a surveillance van about half an hour before you got here. But that's silly, I guess," I said as if to myself. "Why would a Mississippi State vehicle be riding up and down our road?" Our rearranging and settling finished, I went out the bedroom door, whistling, "The All-Seeing eye is Watching You," while Cletus taped paper bags over the windowpanes.

"Evangeline!" Mama called, interrupting me in mid whistle. I suspect she called me that way, not just because it was my name, but judging from her tone of voice, she had been somewhere in the vicinity of Cletus's room a few minutes before. "Yes, Mama?" I answered, arranging my face in its most innocent and appealing expression. If honey could really drip from words, I would've had a whole comb attached to that "Mama."

"Evangeline," Mama continued, totally oblivious to my pious expression, "you oughtn't to plague your poor old Uncle Cletus that way."

"But, Mama," I crooned, "I really did see a van earlier, and I thought maybe Uncle Cletus was right, and you and Daddy weren't being fair, and I wanted him to know somebody in the family really believed in him, and I wouldn't want to do anything to upset poor old Uncle Cletus; I love him more than . . ."

"That's enough, Evangeline. The Word says to let the law of kindness be on your lips. Now leave Uncle Cletus alone." Mama walked off shaking her head and muttering something about the sins of the fathers. I continued whistling and went to see what Daddy was up to. At 205 pounds, and standing six-foot, two, he should have been a rather imposing figure. His Irish heritage lent him a ruddy complexion and twinkling blue eyes stationed above pudgy Santa Claus cheeks. He was almost always smiling, so his pudgy cheeks were in constant evidence, doing away with much of his potential imposingness. Daddy and I were cats out of the same litter, Mama always said, and we spent a lot of time together. Daddy had been a construction worker most of his life, but after he fell off a scaffolding and crushed the bones in the foot he landed on, he was forcibly retired. He took his crippled foot as a blessing in disguise, and decided to live his lifelong dream of having a piece of land all his own and doing a little farming and a little ranching. Except for a limp, his foot didn't hinder him too much from doing his version of farm work, which included a lot of time spent planning. Perhaps I was a bit hasty in putting Daddy on the side of all that's normal. While he is, in my opinion, sane, he is far from most people's conception of normal. I believe Daddy is cognizantly bizarre. He just cares very little about what has been defined as normal or correct, and even less about the opinions of others. When Daddy bought his land, the first thing he did was put up a double gate, then chain and padlock it. That would be reasonable to the most persnickety upholder of averageness except for the fact that it was a good two years before he got around to fencing the property. The gate just sat there guarding the gravel drive with acres of flat, unfenced pastureland stretched out on either side of it. Daddy didn't see that as particularly peculiar, so you can see what I mean. I see it as only fair to mention at this point that all the "sane" relatives branched out from Mama's side of the family, while the opposing camp relatives were Daddy's blood relations, but I still say Daddy belonged with us.

Anyway, I caught up with Daddy out in the south pasture trying to catch up with one of the goats he had bought to keep from having to cut the grass with the riding lawn mower he had bought to keep from having to spend money on a tractor. So far, he had tried cows, the stubbornest horse known to the Free World, and fourteen imported Anconian hens he had bought to keep from having to buy Easter egg dye (the hens laid colored eggs— theoretically). When all those turned out to be more trouble than help, he decided Nubian milk goats had to be the answer. It seemed, however, Nubian milk goats were far more proficient at getting out of fences and consuming cultivated shrubbery than they were at lawn mowing or producing Nubian milk.

"Daddy, Uncle Cletus is here," I said with what I was sure was a conspiratorial air. "Hey, Vangie," he said as he cornered Wilhelm (the goatiest goat of them all), "did he bring any of the little people?" Daddy said the little people were responsible for all the things Cletus imagined happened to him. Mama didn't approve, so we tried to keep allusions to them to a minimum when in her presence. Mama was nowhere in sight now, so I said, "No,

Daddy, but he brought a whole string of government agents, and an extra-terrestrial may be in his suitcase." I thought that was about the funniest thing I could have said, but Daddy must have been too busy putting that rope around the goat's neck to appreciate it. He said for me to help him get the goat back in the pasture, then go with him to gather the squash.

That was about the worst thing he could have said, because Wilhelm was one mean goat and, though I never admitted it to anybody, I was scared of him. I secretly named him Hitler and spent a lot of time figuring out assassination plots. Hitler hated me as much as I hated him and he never failed to try to butt me or scrape me with his nasty old curved horns. But there was no disobeying Daddy, so I grabbed hold of the rope and tried to drag the lock-kneed goat dictator back to the pen to rejoin Gretchen, Helga, and Hannelore. He wouldn't budge, so I leaned forward and pulled with all my might, determined not to let him get the best of me. He suddenly took just a little leap forward and sent me sprawling in the dirt as he pranced past, grazing my arm with one cloven devil hoof. I'd almost swear he was grinning as he caught up to Daddy and let him grab the rope just as docile as can be.

Daddy just looked at me, and I didn't try to explain that Wilhelm had done it on purpose. He might think I had more in common with Uncle Cletus than a last name.

"Daddy," I said a while later as we walked between rows of greenery shot through with big yellow crooked-neck squash, "are you happy being retired and all?" Daddy stopped, pushed his cap back, and wiped his forehead with the blue-and-white bandana he kept tucked in his coverall pocket. He stood squinting up at the hot July sun, and I didn't know if he was deep in thought or looking for signs of rain. I just waited, scrunching my toes into the warm black earth.

"Vangie, I always wanted a little bit of land and the chance to be my own boss, nothing but God and the seasons to direct me,"

Daddy said. "Most times, I'm happy about getting it, but sometimes I miss Booger and Ledbetter and the rest of the boys. I miss the construction sites and having to be somewhere." He shifted positions, tucking his bandana back into his pocket, then smiled, crinkling the corners of his eyes and dispelling the seriousness of the moment. "The worst thing about being retired, Vangie, is there's no breaks."

"Aw, Daddy."

We continued picking squash, moving methodically up and down the rows in a comfortable silence. When we got back to the house, Aunt Lavinia and Uncle Calvin had arrived, complete with François, the ever present, champagne colored poodle—devoid of any semblance of intelligence or purpose—as necessary to Aunt Lavinia as her flower-laden pillbox hat.

Aunt Lavinia is on the saner side of crazy, but terminally ignorant, never meant to actually converse. When she does speak, she displays vast quantities of misinformation, liberally sprinkled with words that bear little resemblance to their original form or meaning. Uncle Calvin is a perfect complement to Aunt Lavinia. He simply doesn't speak, but, rather, grunts answers when faced with direct queries, and spends most of his time reading books and eating peanuts. At any rate, they had arrived.

"Hey there, Aunt Lavinia, Uncle Calvin," I said, stooping to pat François on his fluffy kinked head, rather more forcefully than necessary. "Hello, Evangeline." Aunt Lavinia straightened her hat and looked with a worried air at a now trembling François who leaned against her right leg. "Uhn," grunted Uncle Calvin. At that moment, Mama emerged from the dark cavern of the front hallway, wearing a distinctly disturbed expression. "Joseph, you have to take me to town." She flung the words at Daddy, wringing her hands and frowning at my bare, dust covered feet. My immediate concern was that my feet had somehow elicited the hand wringing, but her next words put that fear to rest.

"Joseph, it's old Miss Stevens. She fell and broke her hip, and I need to go see about her. She don't have any people anymore, and she asked the folks up at the hospital to call me. I've got your car keys here. Evangeline, I've got supper started; see to it. Lavinia, Calvin, I'm sorry to run off and you just getting' here and all. Lavinia, I have to ask you to see to Evangeline and Cletus for me. I don't plan to stay but a while; I might have to go back a spell every day, though, and check on her. You know Dorothy Stevens, Lavinia, up on Cedar Street; Doctor Stevens's sister. Calvin, good to see you. I'll be back after supper some time. Joseph, let's go!" This last she barked emphatically, although all that had prevented them from leaving already was Mama's own torrent of instructions and explanations.

"If you're waiting on me, you're backing up, Emily," Daddy said, but one look from Mama put his sense of humor in a holding pattern. "Lavinia, Calvin." Daddy nodded his head at them as he spoke, then accompanied Mama to the old red Ford she refused to learn to drive. I went on in and stirred the peas and looked at the roast and cornbread in the oven, then sat down at the kitchen table to drink a glass of tea.

"Evangeline," Aunt Lavinia said, "does your mama plan for us to use the bedroom next to yours again?"

"Yes, Ma'am; we put clean sheets on the bed this morning."

"Calvin," she said, airily, "let's go up to our Bedouin to unpack and settle in. Then I'll come down and get us all fed." Uncle Calvin's "Uhn" was just a little louder than usual, but I nearly turned blue and spit tea all over the table trying not to laugh. After a sumptuous feast, in spite of the cornbread, which resembled a thick, dark brown Frisbee (I forgot about it while Aunt Lavinia was unpacking her Arab), we cleaned up and went into the living room to watch television. Cletus, taking no part in kitchen detail, had already settled his considerable bulk into the soft, rust colored, oversized armchair, and was immersed in the world of commercials (which represented Truth to him).

43

"Yeah, that Diet Rite'll shore take it off of you," he said as we entered. "Calvin, gimme some of them peanuts; Girlie, git me a Co Coler." When I returned with the "Co Coler," Aunt Lavinia, Uncle Calvin, François, of course, and Cletus were involved in *Peyton Place*, right where they found out Rachel was abused by her Uncle Jack. It seems the abuse might even have included. . . "Evangeline!" Aunt Lavinia had just noticed my presence in the room, and obviously feared impending moral decay. "Why don't you go get a nice book to read, Lamb. And take a bath. And put on your nighties."

"Yes Ma'am, Aunt Lavinia." I happened to have a copy of *Lady Chatterley's Lover* that Mary Beth McClendon had snitched from her father's library. We had high hopes for it, but I had yet to begin reading it. I decided to combine instructions one and two, and was neck deep in a steamy bath reading the part in chapter two where Connie and Clifford move into Wragby and begin writing stories. I was puzzling over *demi vierge* when the phone rang. I went, dripping, out the bathroom door to answer it, but Aunt Lavinia managed to leave the Carsons long enough to get it first. "God Almighty!" rang out from the downstairs hallway. I moved closer to the stairway. "Are you hurt? Lord above, Joseph. No, you just stay there with her. I'll send Calvin with some things for you both, and I'll tend to everything here. Don't worry about a thing. You just take care of Emily. Will they let you sleep in her room?"

By this time, I had thrown a nightgown over my damp body, and had made it down the stairs. "Evangeline," Aunt Lavinia said upon seeing me standing there staring at her, "your mama and daddy had an accident on the way to the hospital." Now up to that point, I had just assumed that Mama had made a deal with God: in exchange for keeping us all on the straight and narrow, she was assured personal safety by way of Divine Intervention. Daddy was a clause in the contract, I suppose. At seeing my shock and disappointment and interpreting it as worry, Aunt Lavinia began to explain to me that Daddy had just had a little bump, and Mama had a broken ankle and had hurt her neck somehow. A truck had pulled out and hit the passenger side. Aunt Lavinia didn't seem too worried, but I asked if Mama was hurt much. I figured, really, that she had whipped her head around so fast to tell Daddy and her guardian angel what she thought of the whole business that she had strained a ligament or something. "Don't you worry, Evangeline," Aunt Lavinia said, "your mama will probably be home in a couple of days. She may not even have to miss any of the celebrations. I'll be right here with you, and so will Uncle Calvin and Uncle . . . Uncle Calvin and me'll take care of you, Lamb." She pulled me close in a lavender-scented hug, cutting off my airflow by burying my face in her Dacron/polyester-bloused bosom.

I pulled away, gasped my appreciation, and went back upstairs to ponder the possibility of life without Mama and Daddy. It didn't take me long to decide there was no possibility of life without them (Mama would straighten it out with God), and a few days in Aunt Lavinia's care could prove interesting. I returned to my book, to find Connie growing restless.

The next morning I awoke to the smell of biscuits a la Lavinia —flat and crusty and perfect for gravy—mingled with the aroma of bacon and coffee. Biscuits, however, soon stepped into the background; the Event, as Mama had termed it when we had The Talk, had changed my life right while I was sniffing bacon. I got dressed and, with a newfound maturity and a sense of vast importance, I descended the staircase and made my entrance. It seemed nobody else noticed the change in my step or the bloom on my cheek, so I whispered my news to Aunt Lavinia. Her eyes glazed over, and she clasped her hands at her breast and gushed, "That's the weeping of a disappointed womb." She seemed about to go on and explain the disappointment to me, so I told her that Mama had already covered that. Before I could wade into the eggs and biscuits she had heaped on my plate, I began to feel even more different; my stomach felt like it was in the process of being sewn to my back.

"Aunt Lavinia," I said, "I don't feel good at all. I'm going back to bed." I went on up and spent about thirty minutes feeling sorry for myself and wishing Mama was around. I didn't feel nearly so grown up as I had when I first went down to breakfast. In fact, I felt pretty little and very much alone. About the time I was ready to move into the crying stage, Aunt Lavinia peeked her head around the doorframe and asked how I was feeling.

"I brought you a little snack, seeins as how you didn't hardly touch your breakfast." She slipped across the room and placed a bed tray on my lap. Sweet hot tea steamed in one of the special Blue Willow china cups Mama had collected week by week at the Better Living grocery store a few years back. Beside it lay two pieces of french toast sprinkled with cinnamon. As I ate, Aunt Lavinia patted my arm. "Thanks, Aunt Lavinia," I said trying to drink in spite of the pat, pat, pat.

"It won't feel so bad for long, Lamb," she said. "You may think you can't intolerate it, but it passes." Then she smoothed back my hair just like Mama does whenever I'm sick, and I almost cried; I sure didn't feel like laughing at her. I was in definite danger of falling prey to sappiness, so I said, "Hey, Aunt Lavinia, you growing any more of those hybrid proboscis you told me about?"

"Yes, Lord!" she said. "I've got 'em coming up all around that big pine tree in my front yard." The vision this spawned restored my spirits somewhat, but for some reason, Aunt Lavinia didn't seem dumb or silly at all. The warmth of the tea had soothed my stomach, so I decided to get up. I went off to find Cletus, figuring that he would help me retain my pre-Event self.

Cletus was in the living room gazing at the TV set with intense interest as Roy Rogers tried to understand what Gabby was saying. Gabby had misplaced his dentures and kept hollering, "Beneeta falsh, beneeta falsh." I found Cletus more interesting than Roy's predicament, so I sat down to watch him watch. He had a way of hooking his index finger over his nose and resting his chin on his thumb, then sort of collapsing his face, so the nose folded over to almost meet his chin, with the mouth lost somewhere in between.

Gabby found his teeth and yelled out, "I said they was beneath the Falls," just as Cletus noticed me watching him. He unfolded his face and turned to look at me. "Girlie," he said, "don't you worry none about your ma and pa. We know it weren't no accident, that truck hittin 'em, but Old Cletus'll take care of it. No, sir, it weren't no accident; but I know their ways, child, I know their ways."

"Uncle Cletus," I began, but feeling unaccountably generous, I bit back the part about the hidden microphones, and finished lamely, "thanks." I went out the back door and saw Uncle Calvin sitting in the back yard swing, reading and eating peanuts. "Uncle Calvin, whatcha reading?" I called out, then plopped down beside him.

"Uhn," he grunted. I decided to see if his grunts varied in accordance with the conversation, so I said, "I like to read, too. Mama and Daddy almost never read, and Uncle Brantley only reads the newspaper."

"Uhn," he grunted again, resting his book on his knees in order to crack a fresh supply of roasted peanuts. "Aunt Lavinia doesn't read, does she, Uncle Calvin?" I continued. "What in the world do you two talk about? You know, Uncle Calvin, I've never really heard you talk to Aunt Lavinia."

"Evangeline," he said in a rumbling, rusty voice that shook me with its unexpectedness. I looked up at him so fast and so hard my eyeballs felt like they had gone on over to the back of my head. "Your Aunt Lavinia was not put on this earth for discourse. Her value lies in the greatness of her heart—a heart of pure gold, unrefined but precious in its purity. Her hands are instruments of love and healing, and in her youth, her freshness and beauty were a balm of Gilead to my tired, disheartened eyes. Though young, I

47

had become hard and cynical, seeing nothing but deceit and hypocrisy around me. Lavinia, in her innocence and ignorance, proved to be my purpose in life. She needed to be protected, guided, and educated. Alas, my attempts at education fell on infertile ground, yielding only a few random mutants. Hoist on my own petard, I abandoned my efforts in that direction and contented myself with protecting her, and find that in so doing, I myself am protected."

I stared, my mouth open slightly, my swinging stilled. Uncle Calvin resumed reading, occasionally feeding peanuts into his mouth and chewing. Feeling close to him, kindred spirits, I said, "I bet you're reading Shakespeare or Tolstoy, huh, Uncle Calvin? I've read some stuff by Hemingway and Poe. My English teacher gave me a whole list of authors she said I should read."

"Uhn." Uncle Calvin continued reading and eating, without so much as a pause. I craned and strained to see the cover of his book, and made a mental note to get something by P.G. Wodehouse the next time I went to the library.

I went up to my room to look up petard and think about the discoveries I had made. I had convinced myself that I had always known there was more to Uncle Calvin than met the eye, when the phone rang. I heard Aunt Lavinia answer it, then I heard her start crying. I knew somehow I shouldn't let her see me, so I squatted down at the top of the stairs where I could hear. "Joseph, what do I tell Evangeline? All she knows is that her mama hurt her neck and broke her ankle. I even told her y'all would be home in a couple of days."

"Aunt Lavinia, you let me talk to my daddy right now!" I yelled, running down the stairs. I grabbed the phone while she just stood there and spluttered. "Daddy," I said, "what's wrong with my mama? I'm not a little baby, and I want to know and . . ." I couldn't talk anymore. I got scared, more scared than I had ever been in my life. All the words kind of clogged up in the back of my throat, and all I could think was that God had no right to go and back out of a contract. Then I started praying, "God, if you let Mama be all right, I'll be nice as pie to Aunt Lavinia. I'll never be a minute's trouble to anybody. I'll even be good to Uncle Cletus." Then I got mad again and said, right out loud, "God, you just fix it, you hear!" I was yelling and Aunt Lavinia took the phone and handed it to Uncle Calvin and grabbed me in her arms and held on tight. I didn't care anymore whether I smothered in her blouse or not, but I sure did wish her arms were Mama's.

Aunt Lavinia started walking up the stairs and somehow I seemed to be going with her, although I couldn't figure out for sure how to make my legs work. She was telling me that Mama had a blood clot on her brain, and she had gone into a coma. They didn't know if she was going to wake up again. Daddy told her, she said, that the doctor didn't see it before, and I think she was explaining how that could happen, but I was trying to tell her how bad and wicked I felt for going around like nothing was wrong when my mama was dying. Finally, she gave up and just kept saying, "Hush, Lamb." Then I gave up and started praying in my mind, "Please, please, please, God."

"Aunt Lavinia," I begged, "take me to the hospital, please." "No, Lamb," she said looking at me real sad-like. "Your daddy said they won't let you in the room with your mama, so it's best if you just stay home." That wasn't fair, but I didn't say anything; I just told her I wanted to be by myself. "I know, Lamb," she said, then left me there, kind of tiptoeing out of the room like I was the one that was sick.

As soon as I heard her banging around in the kitchen, I slipped down the stairs and got my bicycle out of the barn and started peddling as hard as I could toward downtown Collins. It was about five miles to the hospital, and my legs and back started to hurt really bad about half way there, but I had to go see Mama and make sure she didn't die. When I got to the hospital, I walked right in and said I needed to get a message to my daddy, and the lady at the desk told me that Mama was in Intensive Care up on the third floor. When I got to the third floor, Daddy was just coming out of Mama's room, so I waited till he turned the corner, then when the nurse wasn't looking, I slipped inside.

Mama was lying on the bed, still and white, and she had tubes in her arms and nose and she was all hooked up to machines. It was the first time I had ever seen her when she wasn't in control of everything and everybody. I didn't much like it. I went over and kneeled down beside her and picked up her hand. "Mama," I said, "you have to get better and come home because things won't be right without you. I love Daddy better than life, but I don't think he can take care of everything like you do." I looked up to see if she was listening, but it didn't look like anything had changed. I started crying again and that made me mad at myself, but I couldn't seem to stop. "Guess what, Mama. It happened today. I got my first period. It was a little scary, but now I guess I'm a woman."

Right then a lot of noises started up in the room, and I thought I had bumped something, but then I realized that one of the machines had changed; where it had had a rhythmic kind of beep, it was just humming now and some kind of alarm was ringing. The door banged open and nurses started running into the room. When they saw me there, they started yelling at me to get out, then Daddy ran in and they yelled at him to stay out and to get me out. I grabbed the side of Mama's bed and started screaming, "Mama, please don't die. Please don't die." Daddy came over and pulled my fingers loose and took me out into the hall. I looked over my shoulder and I knew it was the last time I would see Mama.

The next thing I knew, I was waking up in my bed at home and I didn't have any idea how I got there. Then I figured I had just had a bad dream and Mama was downstairs cooking breakfast. I wondered if Uncle Cletus and Uncle Calvin and Aunt Lavinia had really arrived or if they just showed up in the dream. When I got out of bed, I realized that at least the part about growing up was true. I felt really happy, and I was determined that I'd make Mama proud of me. I never realized before that I loved and needed her so much. I took a bath and got dressed as quick as I could, then I went down the stairs so fast I don't think I even touched the steps. When I got to the kitchen, Aunt Lavinia was at the table drinking coffee and looking like she didn't sleep so good. "Aunt Lavinia, you *are* here," I said. She looked at me real funny then put her arm around my waist and told me I needed to get dressed to go to the funeral home. "Funeral home?" I asked. "Why, for who?" She jumped, then started crying, and I just sat down real slow. It wasn't a dream. My mama wasn't cooking breakfast and she never would again. She'd never smooth my hair when I was sick, and she'd never ever smile and call me her "little dickens."

When it came time for the funeral, I refused to look at Mama. I didn't want to see her dead. When they said it was time for the family to walk by the casket, I just sat in my chair, gripping the arms, and shook my head. Then I closed my eyes and remembered Mama teaching me how to make teacakes. After a while, Daddy said we had to go to the chapel, and I went, but I still closed my eyes and remembered Mama so I wouldn't hear what Brother Browne, our pastor, was saying. At the cemetery, I looked away from the casket and the gaping hole in the ground and stared hard at a row of trees and tried to think about how Mama had climbed right up with me in a big oak tree in our back yard when I was in second grade. I guess I was crying, because I could taste salt and feel the water kind of tickle my lip before I wiped it away.

The next day was Sunday, and Daddy's birthday. The party had been canceled, but everybody was going to homecoming at church. Even Daddy, who hadn't been to a homecoming with Bro. Delphi Browne in three years. I could smell chicken frying and knew Aunt Lavinia was fixing what Mama had planned to take for dinner on the grounds. I told Daddy I didn't feel up to going. "You be all right by yourself, Vangie?" he asked. "You want me to stay with you?" I said no, I'd be fine, and he just nodded and walked out. I didn't plan to ever go back to church. I didn't have anything to say to a god who could behave like that. When I heard Uncle Calvin's car pull out of the drive, I went outside and climbed up onto the low limb on the giant oak tree and just sat there staring up at the sky.

When they came back from church, Daddy told me Uncle Calvin and Aunt Lavinia were going to stay on to help out. Uncle Calvin said there wasn't much sense in him going back to his apartment, now that the FBI knew where it was. None of it mattered to me. I just kept trying to make myself believe that this couldn't be true. It didn't feel real. I kept thinking that any minute I'd see Mama and everything would be all right, but at the same time I knew that wasn't going to happen. I spent the next week either in my room or out back in the oak tree. Daddy didn't ask me to help with the chores and Aunt Lavinia took care of everything in the house. I just wanted to be by myself and think. I missed Mama more than I ever thought I could. I'd think of things I wanted to tell her, and I would almost start downstairs when I'd remember that she wouldn't be there. Most of the time Daddy let me eat in my room, because it was hardest of all to go sit at the table and have everybody there but Mama. Sometimes I was mad at Mama for dying, and sometimes at Miss Stevens for asking her to go to the hospital, and sometimes at Daddy for letting Mama go, and always I was mad at God, because He could've done something about it all. Daddy tried to talk to me about Mama dying and all, but he would get so sad and act so hurt that I would tell him I didn't want to talk about it and that I would be fine, just so that look in his eyes would go away. Aunt Lavinia tried too, but I didn't want to talk to her about Mama. I just wanted to talk to Mama again.

One night, Daddy said I'd have to start coming down to the table, because it was too much trouble for Aunt Lavinia to have to wait on me like she was doing. I thought it was wrong of Daddy and selfish of Aunt Lavinia, but that night I went down to supper. Daddy, Uncle Cletus, and everybody were sitting there, everybody but Mama. I felt a big lump in my throat. Aunt Lavinia put a plate on the table for me. "I'm so glad you came down, Lamb," she said. I sat down and tried to eat with everybody staring at me like I was one of the two-headed bullfrogs I had seen in the Freak Tent at the State Fair last spring. After we ate, Aunt Lavinia brought out my favorite dessert, lemon icebox pie. I felt another lump in my throat, but I couldn't tell if it was for Mama or Aunt Lavinia.

The next Sunday everybody got up and got ready for church, but, again, I told Daddy I wasn't feeling good. He looked at me for a long time, but then he said I could stay home. After they left I went out to the oak tree again and stayed there wondering how they could just go into church like God hadn't lied to them. I started talking to God, not praying, just telling Him what I thought. "God," I said, "My Mama always said you loved her and you loved me and you wouldn't let anything bad happen to us. You lied to her, God, and then you killed her and I can't forgive you for that." I got scared a little because I was smartin' off to God, but then I got mad again because what I said was true. He had lied to her and she had lied to me. She was dead and I would never see her again.

"Vangie." For a minute, I thought God had showed up and I was in big trouble, but then I realized it was Daddy standing at the foot of the tree.

"Daddy, you nearly scared the bejeebers out of me. I thought you were . . . at church."

"I decided we needed to have a talk, Vangie. You want to come down?"

"If it's all the same to you, I think I'd rather stay up here."

"Suit yourself." Daddy pulled over the old lawn chair I kept under the shade of the tree and took off his tie and loosened his collar. "Now, Vangie, you know I don't hold too much to church and a lot of church folks."

"I know, Daddy," I interrupted, "and I agree with you. In fact, I think God . . ."

"But," Daddy interrupted right back, "I do hold to the Man Upstairs. Me and Him got an understanding."

I felt the blood shoot to my head again, and heard myself almost yelling, "An understanding? How can you understand God killing Mama?"

"I'm not talking about Mama. I just mean the Good Lord knows I believe in Him, and I count on Him. I just don't care much for visiting Him in the church house with a bunch of hypocrites. And some good, genuine believers," he hastily added, "like your mama."

"But, Daddy, aren't you mad at Him right now?"

"No, Vangie, I'm not. I asked Him about it and all right after she died, and I guess He answered me with my own memories. I got to thinking about how your mama loved that song, "Beulah Land." She used to sing it all the time. And sometimes she'd talk about it. Heaven, I mean. Her whole face would just kinda light up when she talked about what it would be like to walk on streets of gold, and visit with Jesus, and ask God all the hard questions. See, Vangie, even Mama didn't understand all God's doin's. I bet you never knew Aunt Lavinia lost a little baby girl years ago. Born perfect, but never took a breath. Now why? Why would God let her be born only to take her away again? Mama never understood that, but it never shook her believin' that God had a reason for it."

I tried to take that in, but Daddy went on. "Maybe He has a reason for this, too, baby. We don't know what it is, but we don't have to know, we just have to trust, like Mama. The way I see it, if God is real and Beulah Land is real, then Mama didn't die. She just moved. And when time comes for us to go, she'll be the first one at the gates waitin' to take us to our new house."

Daddy stood up then, and started walking toward the back door. I stayed in the tree and thought about what he said. I don't know how long I stayed, but at some point I heard what sounded like the softest singing. I looked around, but I didn't see anybody, so I got real quiet and just sat there listening. I had to close my eyes and strain to hear it. I started to cry again when I realized it was "Beulah Land." I guess Daddy was playing that record of Mama's. I listened real close so I could hear the words. Was Mama in Beulah Land? It didn't seem like Mama would ever have fallen for a bunch of hogwash, so maybe it was true. And if that was true, then so was what Daddy had said. Mama had just gone on ahead, maybe to get all the rooms aired out for us one day.

I jumped down out of that tree and went and got Mama's old, worn Bible from the coffee table where she had been reading it that morning she went to the hospital. I didn't want to waste the time going up to my room. I looked in the back and found all the verses I could about Heaven and everlasting life. When I turned the dog-eared pages to the first verse, it was underlined. So was the next one, and the next. Every verse I found, Mama had been there before me, marking it as special.

I remembered Mama telling me that God had created us so that we could be His family, then Adam sinned and had to move away from God and God was really hurt by it. He loved us and could hardly wait for us to come home. That made me wonder if maybe while Mama was here and away from Him, God had felt like I did now that she was gone away from me. I still wasn't sure about it all, but if it was true, then He hadn't lied and He hadn't killed her; He had just let her come home early because she wanted to see Beulah Land so bad. I wanted to believe it, and I wanted to see Mama again. I wanted to be the kind of person she was and I started praying, crying so hard only God would have been able to understand what I said.

I heard the car pulling back in, so I put the Bible back and went upstairs to wash my face. When I came back down, I went in the kitchen to help Aunt Lavinia get lunch ready. She didn't say anything, just hugged me and told me to put ice in the glasses while she finished frying the last of the Anconian chickens Mama had put in the freezer. We all sat down and I reached over and squeezed Daddy's hand while he asked God's blessing on our meal. My heart and throat felt so full I had trouble swallowing. "Girlie," Cletus said, "pass me them mashed taters." He pointed out their location, sending aromatic fumes wafting my way. I remembered last summer when we were all eating and I had leaned over to smell the flower arrangement in the center of the table. "I was watching a movie one time," I had said then, "where these guys hid microphones in the flowers in this other man's house. They could hear everything that went on. Where you going, Uncle Cletus?" I had asked because Cletus had grabbed his plate and headed out the back door. "Evangeline," Mama had said, and I suspected I knew why she called me that way.

She wouldn't be calling me that way again. She wouldn't be here, but she had spent her time with me trying to teach me and show me how to love others, even the unlovable. I had never understood. Now all I could think was how kind Mama had always been to Cletus, how kind she had been to everyone. "Unto the least of these," she had always said. Now I remembered the verse where Jesus told his Disciples, "When you give even a cup of water to the least of these, you give it to Me." She loved Uncle Cletus as one of the ways she loved Jesus.

I passed Uncle Cletus the potatoes. He dropped the spoon and sent potatoes flying in all directions when I said, "I love you, Uncle Cletus."

In my mind I added, "God, if you're really there, and if it's not too much trouble, will you tell Mama I'm trying to be kind?"

The tiny pink rosebud, dried and placed in the matchbox on a bed of pink satin, makes my heart squeeze. I remember how I thought it would stop altogether the day I put the matchbox in the Sampler. The bud is from Mama's favorite climber. I took a bouquet of them to her funeral to focus on during the interminable service that I wanted to both end, so I could leave, and go on forever so the reality of life without her could be postponed.

Even now, I don't like to think about that time, so I put the match box carefully in the Sampler and move my mind away from that day. When I reach back into the memories, hoping to pull a happier one, my hand closes over a red satin ribbon with silver bells. I jingle the little bells, allowing my mind to close over the sadness like water in a pond after a stone has sunk into its depths. When the surface is smooth again, I can move on.

The Christmas bells. They were a prize won in Sunday School when I was seven. I was the only one able to recite the entire Christmas story from St. Luke. I had hung that ribbon, now frayed and faded, on my bedroom doorknob every Christmas until I left home. The Christmas story competition took place the same year Mama took over as the family holiday hostess. Christmas dinner before that was at Granddaddy and Granny Sullivan's, Mama's grandparents. After breakfast and presents at our house, we would head for their farm and the huge gathering of aunts, uncles, and cousins. On Christmas night, we would go to Aunt Tiny's and have another Christmas dinner with Daddy's side of the family. Granny Sullivan died in the spring of the year I got the bells, and everybody on both sides of the family started coming to our house for holidays. I remember the Christmas before Mama died.

ANOTHER CHRISTMAS STORY

Christmas morning dawned—mornings have a way of doing that—cold and clear. Fifteen or twenty various and sundry relatives had gathered to aid in the festivities. I, for one, thought we could manage quite nicely on our own, but my voice was of little consequence in the family, so gathered they had, and at this moment were congregated in the living room, garbed in an amazing assortment of nightwear, casting furtive glances toward the dining table, and looking for all the world like comic-strip vultures.

Uncle Cletus was moving the couch away from the window to prevent the neighbors from spying on him, and Uncle Brantley was spitting chew into Mama's brass planter, occasionally using one red and white fleece sleeve to wipe a thin brown stream from the corner of his mouth. Close to the dining room sat Uncle Jules and Aunt Lavinia. He was telling her and telling her and telling her the exact method for grafting two varieties of peach trees, and she was craning her neck around the door frame sniffing the aroma of biscuits exuding from the kitchen. I was going around switching coffee cups on everybody when they weren't noticing and trying to memorize the different ways of registering surprise. I planned to be an artist, even though Mama said proper ladies grew up to raise proper families, and I thought it might come in handy. Mama came in just as I was trading Uncle Calvin's one sugar, two creams for Jessie's three sugars, one cream and made me help get breakfast on the table.

I put the last dish on the linen tablecloth we used for company, said, "Breakf. . . " and everybody was sitting at the table— everybody except uncle Brantley; he had to get rid of his chew. I didn't eat much because I was watching how everybody else went about it. Aunt Lavinia opened her teeth wide for a good clamp, put food in, then puckered up when her teeth came back together, and she chewed and chewed each bite before she jutted her head out like a turkey looking over a log and swallowed with an audible gulp. Uncle Jules would take a bite, chew fast, swallow, tell whoever hadn't gotten to the table fast enough to avoid sitting by him how the particular food should have been cooked, then suck his teeth in preparation for the next bite. Uncle Cletus didn't have his teeth in, so he ate soft foods like the eggs and biscuits and gummed them with a soft smacking sound—like the sound you make when you fluff up a feather pillow. The rest of them had unimaginative styles, so I went in to see how the younger relatives were doing. They had been relegated to the kitchen to keep them out of the adults' hair.

When I got there, I could see Mama was going to have conniption fits if I didn't do something. The first thing I did was get Jimmy Joe off the refrigerator and wipe the eggs and grits off his face and out of his hair. His opponents in the food fight that had ended when I came through the swinging door voluntarily began to clean up their ammunition, mostly by scooping it off the table and back onto their plates. The stuff on the floor was deemed inedible even by their standards, so I made Carrie and Suzanne clean that up so I could run the mop around. When the kitchen looked like a kitchen again instead of the set of "War of the Worlds," I gave them all some cherry bombs and told them cows were deaf, and they headed out for Uncle Jules's pasture full of registered Angus.

With the warring factions gone, the kitchen seemed extra quiet, so I just stood there and enjoyed it. It didn't last long, though. In a few minutes, I heard Mama blessing somebody out good. Since it wasn't me this time, I slipped into the living room to find out who was on the receiving end. It was Uncle Brantley. He was learning the difference between a spittoon and a flower pot.

The rest of the adult crew was still stationed at the table, either paying tribute to the breakfast or just passing time until the next feeding. Granddaddy Sullivan had just come downstairs and sat at the table with coffee and a biscuit. He was the last one up, but at least he was wearing something more respectable than fleece robes and flannel nightgowns. I sat down beside him and watched Uncle Cletus across the table. I started trying to imitate the way his face kind of sunk in and folded over when he was absorbed in delusions of grandeur or whatever he thought about. I was working on getting my upper lip to fold over my chin when I noticed Grandpa looking at me. He got up and started toward the kitchen, then motioned for me to follow him.

When we got to the back door, I decided to tell Granddaddy about the cherry bombs. I don't know if I wanted to confess or see if I had his approval, but I told him as we put on our jackets. Granddaddy stepped out on the back porch, tapped François on his hind quarters and said he thought I might not should have sent the kids to the pasture, then he started telling me about the time Uncle Carl stole the rooster from Miss Moffatt.

"You probably don't remember him, but you call to mind I had an older brother named Carlton? We called him Carl," Granddaddy said. "I remember this one time when things was pretty scant at our house. We was poor at best, and it happened we was at worst right then. Well, Carl, he went out and hooked a piece of corn on the end of some fishing string and set out. He ended up in Mount Olive at a farm owned by a couple of spinster ladies, sisters. The chickens in those days weren't much better off than the folks. There wasn't much feed to be had, so they were turned out in the yard to scratch. Old Carl, he went up in the yard a piece and threw that corn out on the ground. A big old Rhode

Island Red gobbled it up and Carl commenced to reeling him in. About that time, the back door opened and out stepped one of the sisters. Carl started running, holding tight to his fishing line, and that big rooster came flapping along behind him, his neck jutting out and his wings straight out, hopping from leg to leg faster than Charlie quit the army. That old lady started running after them both, hair rollers flying ever which-a-way, yelling, 'He won't hurt you, mister, he won't hurt you.'"

Granddaddy cocked his head sideways and started to laugh. I laughed, too, but I was thinking about Uncle Jules's white leghorn hens strutting around not a mile from where we stood.

We walked on a way. Granddaddy watched the road and I watched Granddaddy. He was fat and tall and he had a habit of running his fingers through his hair, so most of the time it stood straight up like Alfalfa on *The Little Rascals*. Granddaddy was Mama's mother's father and he turned ninety-one last September. Ninety-one is pretty old when you think about it, but with Granddaddy you just never thought about it. He didn't seem old in the way you'd expect. He took me fishing every year, and last summer when we went to see him, he had to climb off the cab of Jessie's truck to visit us. He had climbed up there to get to the peach tree so Aunt Lina could bake us a peach cobbler. He did quit driving though. On his eighty-ninth birthday, he drove the old Henry J into town for one last spin. Said it was getting to where he couldn't see good enough to drive. Before that, he used to like to drive as fast as he could, which wasn't too fast in a Henry J, but still when we'd go over hills, my stomach would fly into my chest on the way back down. He'd whiz past stop signs and yell, "S-T-O-P; Spit Tobacco On the Police!"

We walked past the Covington Missionary Baptist Church Memorial Gardens, and I looked over at the rows of tomb stones. Granddaddy looked at me kind of somber and asked, "Evangeline, do you know how many dead people there are in that graveyard?" I couldn't even imagine; all I knew for sure was Alvin

Carmichael's Aunt Eleanor, so I admitted it. "No, sir," I said, wondering how it was that he knew, but never doubting for a moment that he did. "Every one of 'em," he yelled, and bellowed laughing again.

I sighted a squirrel opening an acorn and Granddaddy and I stopped to watch. "Hey, Granddaddy, how come Uncle Cletus is —you know, the way he is?" I asked, scuffing my shoes along in the dust of the road when we started on again.

"Well, I reckon it was partly just born in him," he said. "Your daddy's family was raised just a mile or so from our place, you know, and we knew all the local younguns pretty good anyhow. Bill always said Cletus was about a half a bubble off level." Granddaddy started to smile, but then looked at me and said, "But that weren't real charitable of him. He was ever a man for a joke, though. Do anything for a laugh. Bill, that is, not Cletus.

"Anyway, I remember one time your Uncle Cletus set fire to the lean-to your daddy and Lavinia had built. They wouldn't let him in, see, so Cletus just lit a match and sot it on fire . . . with them in it. He never did think first. His eye got shot out with a BB gun when he was a teenager and he was always a little embarrassed because it crossed whenever it had a mind to, and he kinda stayed to hisself more and more. Then when he was seventeen, he started getting real thick with Louella Jenkins. She was fat and she stunk, but I reckon he loved her. They started talking about getting married."

"I never knew he was married," I said, struck with wonder. What kind of girl would fall for Uncle Cletus?

"I never said he was. I said they was talking about it." Granddaddy took a pouch of Beechnut out of his pocket and stuffed a wad of it into his left cheek.

"You better stay away from Mama's flower pots," I said.

Granddaddy just looked at me and then spit tobacco juice onto the road, making the dust fly up around it. I was watching the dust swirl and sparkle in the air when Granddaddy got back to Cletus's story. I had pretty much forgotten about him, but I tried to look interested.

"About two months after Cletus and Louella came to an understanding, Louella went into Magee to look for a wedding dress. She was crossing the road to Ed Granger's store when a big wagon came barreling around the corner headed straight for her."

"And she got run over and died and Uncle Cletus has never been the same since . . . ," I gushed, my interest renewed by the romance of the tale. Uncle Cletus was a tragic figure. I could hardly wait to get back and pour his tea and mop his brow. I didn't even mind if he called me "girlie."

"No," Granddaddy said. "Cletus was driving the wagon. He swerved to avoid Louella and the wagon tipped over and spilled him out—head first—right up against a creosote fence post. He was out for better'n a day. When he come to, he was like he is now. Louella kind of lost interest and finally married Jake Calhoun and they moved up to Arm."

Granddaddy started whistling *Old Black Dog*, and I stuffed my hands in my pockets and we headed back home.

When we got to the house, most everybody had gone off outside or upstairs except Mama, Daddy, Aunt Tiny, Uncle Calvin, and Aunt Lavinia. We went on in the living room with them and sat down on the couch side by side. After a while, Granddaddy noticed me looking intently at Uncle Cletus. He smiled a little, patted me on the shoulder, and asked softly, "Thinking about what I told you, Evangeline?"

"Yes, sir," I said. "Do you think chickens would eat Indian corn?"

I suppose I was a disappointment to Granddaddy, as I resisted his attempts to mold my character. But it was a bit of a case of the pot calling the kettle black, as I heard over the years of the practical jokes he and his brothers liked to play. Apparently this aspect of our personality was a dominant trait in the Sullivan gene pool.

My fingers brush against a hard dry peach pit when I delve into the Sampler box and I take it out with mixed feelings, rolling it in my palm. Rella McDonald and peaches are bound up inextricably in my mind.

THE ZUCKERMAN INCIDENT

Rella McDonald collared me and Daddy when we passed her house on the way to Granddaddy's. Miss McDonald talks real low and harsh and her eyebrows are always scrunched together over little light gray slits of eyes that dart around here and there and everywhere except the face of the person she's talking to. She's tall and skinny and kind of hunched over. Her face is brown with deep wrinkles and her skin is tough looking like the naugahyde on the couch in Helen Horton's living room. She chain smokes and talks about Jesus. When Daddy saw her coming out the front door, he started walking faster, but not fast enough.

"Morning, Joseph," she called, waving him over to her front gate then striking a match on the fence post to light a cigarette.

"Morning, Rella," Daddy said. "You remember Vangie."

"Vangie," she said and nodded to me as she grabbed Daddy by the arm and pulled him away. "Best not talk too free in front of children," she said in that voice that sounded like she had a load of pea gravel in her throat. When she was about four feet away, she leaned in toward Daddy, although she was glaring at the dogwood tree beside him, and spoke confidentially in a voice that carried perfectly well to where I was standing.

"You know, Joseph, you'll want to watch that girl of yours. She oughtn't to be running around like a wild thing day and night."

"Rella," Daddy interrupted, obviously annoyed, "Vangie don't run around day and night, and she certainly isn't let loose like a wild thing."

"I mean no disrespect," Miss McDonald said, using the small stub of her cigarette to light another one. She dropped the pack back in the large front pocket of the orange and yellow flower-print duster she wore with stretch pants and red Grasshopper shoes with white ankle socks. "But since the Zuckerman incident. . . ." She actually looked Daddy dead on in the face when she said Zuckerman, with her mouth pursed liked she'd tasted something nasty.

"Now, Rella, you don't really think Sid Zuckerman is a threat to anybody?"

"Sid Zuckerman is lower than the fleas on a dog's belly," Miss McDonald ground out. "You know what he did, Joseph. And how you can stand there and defend him is beyond me." Miss McDonald got so worked up when she was saying this that she threw her arms out and sent her Winston Menthol flying into the pine straw under her camellias. She got down on her hands and knees, still fussing. "Our little girls aren't safe to walk around by themselves," she said, scattering the straw. "And our boys should be kept well away from the likes of . . . Zuckerman." She zeroed in on Daddy's nose this time. When she looked back down, she spotted smoke coming up near a tree trunk and grabbed the cigarette, slapped it between her lips, and stomped on the lightly smoldering straw.

I viewed this as a tactical diversion and inched closer to Daddy, so I would be sure not to miss anything in case she actually lowered her voice.

"I always knew he was trouble," she continued, "ever since Bo and Loretta took him in off the street." She shook another Winston out of the pack.

"They didn't take him in off the streets like a hobo, Rella. He was Bo's nephew, and Bo was Sid's only living relative when his mother died. You know that."

Miss McDonald took a long, deep draw off the cigarette, her eyes squinched up even smaller than before, then let the smoke out through her nose. "Well, I think his brain turned when his mama got struck with . . . The Cancer." She lowered her voice reverentially when she said The Cancer. "That's what I think. He skulked around that big old house, didn't help Bo with the farm work. He was useless as tits on a boar hog." She took another draw. "He didn't run around with the other boys. He was a socialpath. That's what he was, a socialpath."

I inched closer still. This was getting really good.

"He had no, what do they call it? Remorse. That's it. After he did what he did, he wasn't one bit sorry. Never saw anything wrong with it."

"Well, Rella. . . "

"No, don't stand up for that piece of white trash. You know I'm right, Joseph Tanner. I don't even want to imagine what Jesus will have to say to him on Judgment Day."

I thought I heard Daddy mutter something about how she'd probably never be anywhere near Jesus, but I can't be sure. Daddy was kind of talking behind his hand, acting like he was wiping his mouth, and I was still a little further away than I wanted. I moved again, as close as I dared, and squatted down so I'd be less noticeable.

"We better get on our way, Rella," Daddy said then. "Elijah is looking for us to come help pick his . . .peaches."

Daddy's voice went low and hesitant on this last word, like he'd hit his thumb nail with the hammer and let slip a cuss word in front of Mama. Miss McDonald paled.

"Are you trying to be funny?" She asked in a growl, and Daddy started backing up. I tried to scramble up, but it was too late. He tripped over me and went sprawling in the dirt. When he got up, his face was redder than his bandana and I figured I'd never live to see tenth grade.

"That's just the truth of it, Rella," he said, grabbing my arm and pulling me up alongside him. "We got to get on over there before Elijah gets the law out looking for us." He looked a little sick as he said this, too, and we started moving on down the road.

Miss McDonald called after us in a voice like tires screeching on blacktop, "Jesus sees all, Joseph Tanner, and he won't take kindly to you being a smartass—forgive me, Lord—to a poor old widder woman who has been rurnt by a lying, thieving, white-headed devil like Sid Zuckerman."

"Daddy . . ."

"Can it, Vangie," Daddy snapped and I knew either I or Rella McDonald had pushed him too far. I didn't say another word all the way to Granddaddy's. I picked peaches as fast as I could, trying to get back in Daddy's good graces. It wasn't until my cousin, Redelle, came out to pick peaches from the tree I was working on that I opened my mouth again, and even then he spoke first.

"You're sure working hard, Vangie. You in trouble?" he asked as he put the plump juicy peaches in the bushel basket. I looked around, ignoring the insult, but Daddy was across the orchard, so I said, "Redelle, do you know anything about the Zuckerman incident?" I unconsciously said Zuckerman almost like you'd say snot.

"Incident? Zuckerman?" Redelle asked, his eyebrows drawn as he thought about it. "No, why?"

"Rella McDonald cornered us this morning and told Daddy that Sid Zuckerman was a devil and none of the children were safe around him," I said, relishing the opportunity to be the bearer of such news. "Do you think he kidnapped somebody? Or worse?"

Redelle thought some more, steadily picking and piling peaches. Finally, he turned to me and said, "Well, he still lives over on the old Parish farm. If he kidnapped or killed, or. . . uh, you know, somebody, he'd be in prison, right?"

"Yeah, that's. . ."

Just then loud laughter bellowed out from behind the trees to our right. I jumped halfway up a peach tree as Granddaddy

Sullivan stepped out, leaning over and holding his considerable stomach. He laughed until I thought he'd have a stroke right there in the middle of the peach orchard. "The Zuckerman incident," he finally wheezed out. "Oh law, that crazy old bat."

When he could stand upright again, I looked at him with what dignity I could muster and said, "Granddaddy, what is so funny about a. . . a molester?"

Well, that set him off again. "Molester. Sid Zuckerman." Finally, he took out the handkerchief from his overalls pocket and wiped his eyes. "Vangie, Redelle, let this be a lesson about listening to and, worse yet, repeating gossip." Grandpa blew his nose loudly into the black and red cloth. "Rella McDonald hired Sid Zuckerman to clean her chimney and sweep off her roof last winter. When he got done, Rella said he tore the shingles up and she wasn't going to pay him. Sid pointed out that she'd been patching that roof for the last ten years and he not only hadn't hurt her roof, he'd pitched some bad places without even telling her just to help her out."

Granddaddy took out his snuff can and put a pinch in his lower lip before going on. "Well she said he owed her for the damage, but she'd call it even on account of he had cleaned her chimney and got all the leaves and straw off the roof."

I didn't see how this endangered the children any and was about to say so when Granddaddy put up a warning hand.

"Sid, he's a cool one, he is," Granddaddy said. "He just let it go and went home."

"But, how is that. . . " Up came the warning hand again, so I shut my mouth.

"Come summer, the peaches got ripe and Rella went to Mount Olive one Monday and hired a bunch of those Foster boys to come pick her peaches the next Saturday. You know she's got the biggest orchard around and her peaches bring a right smart. When they showed up and Rella took them to the orchard, there wasn't one peach to be seen. Not nary a one, ripe or otherwise.

71

"Rella stood there for a while, Jack Foster said, with her mouth hanging open, then she lit out for the house yelling like a banshee about Sid Zuckerman. Called him a thieving devil."

Granddaddy spit a long stream of dark brown juice onto the grass. "She called the law and tried to have him arrested, but there was no sign of any peaches at his house and nobody had seen him anywhere near her orchard. But Sid walked around town looking real satisfied for a while and pretty shortly he painted his front porch and bought some new rocking chairs and a Black Angus bull. Came into a little money somewhere, I reckon." Granddaddy spit again and turned to go back to the trees where he had been picking. Then he turned around, smiled, and said, "Sid named that bull Peaches."

I smile and lie back on the wedding-ring quilt that has adorned my bed for what seems like forever, but I imagine it is actually the fruit of Aunt Lavinia's sewing circle. The bone-deep exhaustion of grief overtakes me and I doze. When I wake up, it is inky black outside my window and I am thinking again about Rella McDonald. There is a song by a new folk artist, Kate Campbell, that says she never dreamed that people outside the culture of the South saw our way of life in Black and White. I relate to that. In my personal world, admittedly insular as I can see now that it was, there was no hate. Either we were not prejudiced at all, or we were prejudiced at the molecular level and didn't even realize it.

But I came to realize that my home was not a microcosm of the South. And the first I understood of prejudice came courtesy of Rella McDonald.

THE LAND OF NOD

"Emily Tanner, what is that *girl* doing coming in your front door bold as brass?" Rella McDonald said in a harsh whisper that was clearly meant to be heard by all, including Mamie Hawkins, the tall, regal colored woman who had just walked in.

Anybody who had been in Covington County more than a week knew Mamie Hawkins. If there was an illness in a family, colored or white, Mamie was the first one there offering to cook, iron, clean, or watch the little ones. Most times, she also had with her some herbal concoction she had made especially for the particular malady. Usually Mamie's salves or syrups were more effective than the pills and potions dispensed at the drug store. In fact, Mr. Henderson, the pharmacist at Collins Drug Store, had been known on more than one occasion to steer a prospective customer down to Mamie's little yellow house out near the Salem community.

"To have cake and coffee, I imagine, Rella," answered Mama, cool as the stream in Granddaddy Sullivan's woods. "Come on in, Mamie. You're late getting here," she called.

Mamie walked across the living room, gave Mama a hug, and kissed my cheek, before taking off her thin sweater and handing it to Miss McDonald, who took it automatically then stood there gaping. Mamie picked up a cup from the dining room table. "I just came from the Pitts' place," she answered. "Those boys got the croup again. I took 'em a mustard and camphor poultice." She poured coffee in her cup while behind her, Rella McDonald, who seemed to me to have turned as still as Lot's wife, came back to life, turned red in the face, and began to sputter.

"Well, I never . . ." she said, then threw the sweater on the floor, spun around, and stormed toward the front door.

"Probably never will, neither," Mamie muttered, then added a generous portion of cream to her coffee, making it much the color of her skin.

Nobody in that room moved or spoke. They all just stared from the door to Mamie to Mama. Mama walked over, picked up the sweater, and hung it on the back of a chair, saying, "How was Buddy Ray, Mamie? I heard he has the gout so bad he can't even walk from the stove to the table." Whatever spell had frozen everybody seemed to break then, and they all started talking again, like a light switch had been flipped off and back on.

I went over to examine the sweater to see what was on it that made Miss McDonald throw it down. Seeing nothing but an ordinary sweater, I shrugged and went outside. I heard one of the men say, "I wonder what was eatin' that old bat?" but paid no attention to the answer as I went to the far side of the porch. I had some roly poly bugs in a coffee can that I wanted to race. But my ears pricked up when Mrs. McClendon came outside and told her husband what had happened.

"Old bigot, treating Mamie like that," Mr. McClendon said.

"Well, now, Ralph, not everbody is as generous natured as we are," said Old Mr. Keller. "Some folks think the coloreds are getting above theirselves."

The coloreds? I never thought of Mamie as colored. Her skin was like a Milk Dud, but I had just thought of her as plain old Mamie until now.

"Our coloreds are just like they've always been," said Brother Delphi Browne, the preacher at Crossroads Missionary Baptist Church. "They're good people and they know their place."

"That's right," murmured some, but Bub Grayson said, "What's their place?"

That made me sit up and take notice. Their place? Did they mean the colored communities?

"Now, Bub, don't get your drawers in a wad. I don't mean nothing bad by that. But that's the way things are," said Mr. Keller.

How are things? I wondered, the roly polies forgotten.

"May be the way things are, but ain't the way they gone stay," added Uncle Wilson.

Terry Trotter spoke up then. "I don't 'spise 'em," he said. "They ain't like us though. The Good Book says there is a race borned to be slaves."

Brother Browne interrupted, saying, "Let's not forget, boys, that that same book says God punished Aaron and Miriam for their attitude toward Moses's Ethiopian wife."

Folks in Mississippi, and my family in particular, almost always brought the Bible into any argument. I think they could have found a verse to support God's view on corn flakes. But still, I figured if God thought so highly of colored people, we best be careful. Terry Trotter didn't say anything right then, but when Brother Browne left a few minutes later, he picked right back up.

"The Bible says the coloreds first come about when Cain ran off after killing Abel. It says that Cain went into Nod, the land of the orangutan, and there he knew his wife," said Terry, nodding for emphasis. "That proves that the colored people are only half human. That's why it ain't right to be mixin' with 'em."

I didn't see how Cain could know his wife when he had just got to Nod himself, but that didn't seem to be the biggest issue for Daddy. "Terry," he said, "show me in the Bible where it says that," and Daddy went in and got our Bible and handed it to him. After reading most of Genesis a couple of times, Terry slapped the Bible down on the porch swing and muttered, "Well, it's in Mama's Bible," then stomped down the porch steps and across the yard.

The men laughed, but there was something different, an uneasiness that had come over them. The easy talk and laughter stopped. I went to find some new roly polies to race, but I kept thinking about how Miss McDonald had treated Mamie. When I went back in for a glass of grape Kool-Aid, Mamie and the other ladies were eating cake and talking like normal, so I figured Miss McDonald was just crazy and I had no time for crazy.

Crazy came on anyway, ready or not. I saw news reports of terrible things, hatred and violence. Although nothing had overtly changed in my life, there was an underlying tension. Doors that had never been locked before were carefully secured. People were just a little wary, a bit on edge. I noticed, but it didn't really affect me personally. Not at first, anyway.

CHANGE

My best friend in Hot Coffee, Mississippi was Willie T. Clifford. Well, after Linda Sue, but she was my cousin, and I'm not sure if cousins can be friends too, so I guess Willie T really was my best friend there.

At least until the summer of 1965. Before that, the first thing I did when we pulled into Aunt Tiny's driveway was jump out of the car and beat feet for the big vacant lot way down the road from the general store. I knew I'd find Willie T somewhere near, and Linda Sue knew I'd be back directly.

Directly is what Daddy always said when he went down to the courthouse to sit and watch the old men while they watched everybody else. "I'll be back directly," he would call, and Mama would let out a little "hmmph" sound. He might come back for dinner or in the middle of the afternoon, or he might not come home until just before supper. The first time I remember hearing him say that was one of those times he didn't get back until suppertime. Mama was pretty put out, banging pans around and muttering. Daddy came in the door, whistling *Get Along Home, Cindy*, and Mama stopped him in the hallway.

"Joseph," she had said then, "you've been gone all the live long day. I thought you said you'd be right back."

"No," Daddy had answered, "I'd said I'd be back directly." He took his boots off then rolled up his shirt sleeves, while Mama stood there patting her foot ninety to nothing, which meant she was madder than a cat in a washtub. Daddy patted her cheek, which just made her madder, then said, "When I got ready to leave,

I came directly back here." He went down the hall to wash up for supper, and Mama said,"Hmphhhh," real loud this time, and stomped off into the kitchen.

Anyway, this visit in June just before my tenth birthday, I jumped out of the car like usual, yelled, "Be back directly," making sure Mama knew it was Linda Sue I was talking to, and ran off down the road toward the general store. When I got to the vacant lot, Willie T was nowhere to be seen. He wasn't at the store, or the creek, or the junk yard, or any of the places I usually could find him. I wanted to see him, but I didn't know if I dared to go any further than the junk yard. It was just a little ways down the road to the quarters. Most people called it the nigger quarters, but Mama told me not to say that. I wasn't allowed to say nigger. Mama said that meant people who were trashy no matter what color they were. If I was talking about colored people, that's what I should say.

I sat down in the grass outside the junkyard fence and thought about what to do. I hadn't seen Willie T since we had come to Hot Coffee Easter Sunday. I wanted to tell him about Scott Simpson asking Carla Kling to be his Valentine instead of me. I meant to tell him on Easter but I had forgotten all about my broken heart because we were playing marbles and eating devilled eggs. There were always lots of devilled eggs at Easter and they were one of Willie T's favorites.

After what seemed like an hour and there was still no sign of Willie T, I made up my mind and marched off toward the quarters.

I had barely gotten over the hill when I saw him playing kick ball in the front yard of a house that looked like most of its paint had been scrubbed off with a Brillo pad.

"Willie T!" I yelled and started running. But Willie T turned, held up his hand like the crossing guard near the school, said something to his friends, and started walking toward me real fast.

"What you doin' here?" he asked. No hello, no I've missed you. No nothing. Just, "What you doin' here?"

"Well, that's real nice, Willie T. What are you so grumpy about?"

"You ain't sposed to be down here," he said and grabbed my arm and hurried me back to the junk yard.

"Let's get a Nehi grape," I said, but Willie T just stopped and stared at me.

"I ain't yo frien no more," he said finally.

I laughed, but he didn't laugh back, so I said, "What are you talking about? Of course, you're my friend. You're my best friend."

"Not no more."

"But, why, Willie T? What have I done?"

"Ain't nuthin' you done. Who you is."

"Who I am?" I asked. "I'm Evangeline Tanner just like I've always been.

"Well what you is then," he said, rubbing his bare toes in the grass and refusing to look at me.

"Because I'm a girl?" I said, straightening my shoulders and glaring hard at him. "That's never bothered you before. I can play marbles and football as good as any boy, and I can climb trees and fish . . ."

"Vangie," he interrupted, looking at me for the first time. "You a white girl."

"Well, Willie T, I've always been a white girl, too."

Before I could get started good, Willie T interrupted me again. "Things is different. I cain't be yo frien. Get me kilt if I be seen wit' you."

"What things are different? We've always been friends and everybody knows it," I said, trying hard not to sniffle.

"Yeah, evabody know it and that why we cain't be friens. My cuzzins are joinin' up wit the Black Panthers and they say we gots to stand up to the white folk and get our civil rights. The white mens be tellin' us we gettin' too big fo our britches and we best be staying in the quarters wit our own kind."

"But that's crazy," I said. "I don't understand. What kind of civil rights are they talking about?"

Willie T reached down for a blade of grass, blew on it, then started chewing on it. "Well," he said, "You know Doc Roberts's office? You been there?"

"Yeah," I said. "I had to get a shot last summer when my poison ivy got infected."

"You 'member they gots two waitin' rooms? One that say 'Colored' on the door?"

"Yeah," I said slowly, trying to recall the doctor's office. "Oh, yeah, I do remember, and one of the water fountains says 'Colored' over it, too."

"Well, that's civil rights."

I was even more confused. "What does the water fountain have to do with you and me being friends, Willie T?"

"Way I understan' it, shouldn't be no separate fountain just for colored folk."

"Well, I don't know why there is, but I don't see what it has to do with us."

"JayJay, he my cuzzin, he say white folks think we not good enough to drink from the same fountain. Think we nasty or sumthin, so we has to have a separate fountain, separate waitin' room. Don't rub off on no white folks. JayJay say civil rights and Black Panthers gone get rid all that."

"Why don't we just ask Dr. Roberts to take the colored signs down? Then we can be friends," I suggested.

"Bigger'n that, Vangie. JayJay say the colored folk tired bein' beat down. Tired a sayin' yassir and nossir to a white man just 'cause he white."

I got quiet because that made me remember a few months ago when I went to the Woolworth in Hattiesburg. Mama wanted me to get her some handkerchiefs, so she let me out at the curb. When I got to the door, an old colored woman was about to go in, and she stopped and opened the door for me. I went in and said thank you and she said, "Yes, Ma'am," and I wondered why she did that. I was just a kid and Mama said I should say Ma'am and hold doors open for older people, not the other way around.

Willie T went on. "JayJay say the white mens not gone let us have our rights without some bloodshed. He say he hate white folk and white folk hate colored folk."

"But that's not true, Willie T. I don't hate you and you don't hate me. My mama told me not to hate anybody."

"That yo mama and daddy. That not evabody mama and daddy. My mama tole me de same thing. She don't hate white folk, but she did say I cain't be yo frien. Say it ain't safe for neither one of us. I cain't even go to the general sto no more. Not cause of Mizz Speed. No, she all right. Some white mens from out in the county, though, dey say dey make trouble for Mizz Speed if she let little nigger boys shop in her sto. My mama say stay out de sto, stay in de quarters, and stay outta trouble."

I was crying like a big old baby now, with my face all wet and my nose snotty. "But, Willie T," I blubbered. "You're my best friend. It's not fair."

"No. Ain't fair. But ain't nuthin' we can do."

"I'm gonna do something," I said, wiping my nose on my shirt tail. "I'm goin back right now to talk to my daddy."

Willie T just shook his head, and that made me mad. "You just gonna give up? Just like that, Willie T? You gonna let something come between us?"

"Sumpthin' already has, Vangie," he said softly. "White skin, brown skin, and dem railroad tracks."

I didn't see Willie T again until I was twenty-two. At my house, we continued to hear about riots and marches and murders in places like Jackson and in Alabama, but things stayed pretty quiet in Collins, Mississippi. Funny thing, civil rights and desegregation did the opposite for us in a lot of ways in the beginning. Because of the fear of trouble, the Blacks stayed on the other side of the tracks for the most part, and the white people had to abandon colored friends or be ostracized. All summer, people quietly dreaded the fall. Integration was coming to the public schools and no one knew what would happen. When I walked in to my seventh-grade English class, there was one black face. Albert Barnes sat right behind me. Nothing happened but grammar. The day went by quietly and then the week, the month, the school year. The tension deflated, the doors unlocked, and life went on as usual, except there were no colored waiting rooms, no separate lines at the Dairy Dream for whites and Blacks. I don't mean to say there were no racial divisions or inequalities. The news was full of unspeakable acts, and I saw my aunts crying more than once as they and Daddy and my uncles quietly talked about the most recent horror perpetrated all in the name of a layer of epidermis. But the hate and the violence that some people associate with the entire South just wasn't a reality for me in my home and in my little circle of family, although I didn't have to travel far outside my front door to find it.

I put the lid on the box, then close my eyes. They burn and my heart hurts. I try to pray, but words bounce off the yellowed ceiling. "Are you listening?" I whisper. Is it counted as faith if you expect an answer to that question?

Growing up, I fought and refought the battle of faith versus logic. My mother's deep conviction in the God of the Baptists was firmly lodged in my mind, juxtaposed with my father's unconventional primitive faith in "the man upstairs," but without any rules, regulations, or operator's manual. Add to that my questioning mind that refuses to accept anything at face value. I have to understand why I should believe something. So from early days, I questioned, and events and inconsistencies conspired to make that "faith of a child" elude me, even as a child.

I remember the last time Daddy went to a church service before Mama's death took him back through those white double doors. It was homecoming at Crossroads Missionary Baptist Church out on Schoolhouse Road.

HOMECOMING AT CROSSROADS MISSIONARY BAPTIST CHURCH

Brother Delphi Browne preached at Homecoming every year at Crossroads Missionary Baptist Church. Homecoming was the anniversary of the church and it meant all-day preaching and singing, and Dinner on the Grounds. It also meant Daddy went to church; he loved good singing and dumplings. Mrs. Delphi Browne made the best chicken and dumplings in Covington, Smith, and Simpson counties combined.

Every year, Ferlon Trenton came to lead the singing, and Mr. Parker sang a special. Mr. Parker's voice was shaky and he forgot the words sometimes, but he still sang a special, 'cause he was old. Usually the red-headed Burleson children—Jeannie, Marvin, and Bo—sang two or three songs. They hated to sing, but their mama made them, so they just stood around the piano looking bored and singing flat. That wasn't the good singing Daddy came to hear; the good stuff came after dinner when gospel quartets from all over Mississippi would sing. Ferlon Trenton had one of the best quartets around; they sang *I've Been Walking* so good it made you want to hug the tenor.

This year, Brother Browne was really preaching. He was in the pulpit walking back and forth, slamming his Bible down on the podium, and yelling and spitting so much his false teeth kept slipping out of place every few minutes. He never let it bother him though; he just said, "'Scuse me," and popped 'em back in place. I was sitting on the edge of my seat, wedged in between

Mama and Daddy, seeing myself on a one-way train to Hell. I was about ready to change my ways and run down the aisle when one last "'Scuse me," brought me out of it. I leaned back and took a deep breath, then looked up at Mama and Daddy to see if they'd noticed me being almost converted and all. Mama was crying too hard to notice much of anything—she was holding her Bible real close with her arms crossed around it—and Daddy was staring at his reflection in old Mr. Thompkins's bald head.

About that time, Brother Browne either got finished or hungry, so everybody sang *Just As I Am*, while the lost and dying were offered one last chance for everlasting salvation. Nobody surrendered, so Brother Richards dismissed us with a word of prayer, and we all went out to dig into those dumplings. Daddy leaned over and whispered, "Vangie, do you think Mr. Thompkins uses Vinyl Wax to shine his head?"

"No," I said, "he uses Kiwi neutral. And then Mrs. Thompkins puts his head on the shoe-shine box and buffs it up." We laughed at the picture that made, but Mama looked at us kind of sad and mad all at the same time, so we figured we better act Godly for a while.

We got out to the big table made of saw horses and three-quarter-inch plywood, and stood looking for a minute at all those dishes of fried chicken, potato salad, ham, butterbeans, field peas, cornbread, cakes, pies, banana pudding, and Sister Browne's dumplings. We started helping our plates, and Sister Browne made sure I got the gizzard. To wash it all down, there were gallon jugs of sweet iced tea and grape Kool Aid. It was almost as good as Christmas.

After dinner, we went back in to listen to Brother Browne. Daddy said it was the price you had to pay for the dumplings and Ferlon Trenton. I was so full of dumplings and banana pudding, I kept going to sleep, but Mama pinched my earlobe every time and I woke up. She didn't want me to miss anything; if I did, I might harden my heart and be given over to a reprobate mind like my cousin Billy Lee who moved to Louisiana and married a woman who ran a beer joint. I started thinking about my birthday—I was going to be eleven in August—and that kept me awake.

Daddy had just had his birthday the day after Independence Day, so he didn't have anything to think about. After a few minutes of hearing how the whale swallowed Jonah because Jonah wouldn't listen to "The Call," Daddy's head eased back against the pew, and he started snoring real soft. I loved to watch Daddy sleep. He didn't make a real loud noise; he just snored deep in his throat with every breath. Then when he let it out, it would kind of lift his upper lip and then flop it back down with a little puffing, plopping sound. I just sat there watching him. Then Mama heard it. She started looking real worried, 'cause he was getting louder and we didn't dare wake him up. See, since he was in the Army, if you woke him up, you had to run real fast, or he'd jump up and act like he was going to hit you. He would have, too, if anybody stayed close enough. Anyway, we didn't neither of us want to wake him up in church.

Brother Browne noticed Daddy's head sticking out in the aisle and he started talking about how we had a Jonah in the congregation. Right here at Crossroads Missionary Baptist Church—a Jonah refusing to listen to the word of God. He said God like GAAAaaad. I sat bolt upright, not a bit sleepy anymore. Mama was wringing her hands and saying kind of breathy, "Please, God; please, God." She was too scared to wake Daddy up, but Brother Browne didn't know Daddy had been in the Army, and he climbed down from the pulpit and walked right down the aisle and stopped beside Daddy's head. He said, "BROTHER Tanner!" He yelled it, and he whopped Daddy on the shoulder with his Bible. "God would h . . ." He didn't get to finish; Daddy hopped up, wild-eyed, and let go with a back-handed slap, right across Brother Browne's left cheek. He knocked one side of his glasses off and loosened his dentures.

"Lord, God!" Mama said. "Joseph, look what you have done." Brother Browne just stood there with his glasses hanging down on one ear and his front teeth pushed out over his bottom ones. He looked like Jerry Lewis in that old movie we saw last winter. Daddy's eyes cleared up and he looked at Brother Browne then at Mama beside him crying. I was standing on the pew so I could see better. Daddy grabbed me down and walked out the door. Mama stayed on to see about Brother Browne and pray for Daddy's redemption.

I don't know if Daddy got redeemed, but he never went to Homecoming again. One time, he did go hear Ferlon Trenton's quartet at a sing over at the Rock of Ages Independent Baptist Church in Mendenhall. Mama cried a lot about Daddy's heathen ways, and she took me to church every time the door opened so I would find the Lord and grow up to be a believer and have no yoke with iniquity. After that, though, I had trouble listening because I kept remembering when Daddy slapped the preacher. It made me laugh, but it also made me start to wonder if maybe Daddy didn't have a better handle on what God wanted from us than Mama and Brother Delphi Browne. I don't mean hittin' the preacher; I mean getting to know God personally. Daddy said his time with God was better spent looking up at the sky or picking tomatoes or sittin' by the river, not in a stuffy church with Sunday clothes, Sunday hairdos, and Sunday attitudes, with a preacher yelling at you about how rotten you are. I did look up reprobate, though—just in case.

I gave Mama a lot of grief about church attendance after that because I agreed with Daddy. I had seen hypocrisy, even though I didn't know the word for it at that tender age, and plus it just felt better to believe in Daddy's version of God. You had a lot more liberty for one thing.

I knew how Daddy felt and I knew what Mama believed. It wasn't long before I discovered there were a lot more questions. It wasn't just about church going. I learned about denominations and division and religious snobbery. Mama would have been greatly surprised to find she lent to my growing questions with simple little inconsistencies like Sunday donuts.

SUNDAY DONUTS

Sundays at our house are spent celebrating the Sabbath. Nobody works on the Sabbath. Saturdays are spent cleaning the house and dressing up the yard. Mama makes me take knick knacks off the wall and wash them while she hauls the mattresses out to the yard to sun. Even Daddy has to participate. Mama has him out mowing the grass as soon as the dew's gone. On Saturday night, I shine my Sunday shoes with a piece of leftover biscuit before I take a bath and wash my hair. If cleanliness is next to Godliness, I guess we're ready to head up to the Pearly Gates any time.

But, then, old Clara Wilcox says Saturday is the real Sabbath and if she's right, we've just scrubbed and dusted our way into outer darkness where there is weeping and gnashing of teeth. Now here's the thing of it. Mama says we owe it to God to show up in His house every time we have an opportunity. Daddy stopped showing up after that time he slapped Brother Browne, but he still reads his Bible and talks to "the Man Upstairs." And if Crossroads Missionary Baptist is God's House, what about the Church of the Immaculate Conception that Linda Eden goes to? Whose house is that?

I heard Aunt Lavinia once saying that the poor Catholics were heathens and we needed to share the Gospel with them, so they wouldn't end up in eternal damnation. Uncle Calvin told her that the idea of any one religious affiliation possessing sole rights to the streets of gold is Convoluted thinking. I don't think we have any Convoluteds in Covington County. All I've ever seen are the

Baptists, the Catholics, the Seventh Day Adventists, and a holiness Oneness bunch out on Seth Johnson Road. Maybe they have a church up in Jackson. I'll have to look that up.

But anyway, I started wondering about the Sabbath. Like I said, Mama won't let anybody do a lick of work on Sunday, but she'll let Daddy take us to the Donut Hole on the way to church. I don't know how it is in big cities, but around here there's something called a blue law that means nobody sells anything on Sunday. If you're going to be doing something dangerous on Sunday, you better get your Band-Aids Saturday night, because you'll be flat out of luck on the Sabbath.

Jamie O'Shea runs the Donut Hole and he's in there seven days a week. Most days he has big old cat-head biscuits and tomato gravy and grits and eggs along with the donuts. On Sunday, there's a big closed sign on the door, but it's not locked. The only thing on the counter up front is donuts and you go in and get what you want and leave the money in a cigar box, like a tip. He never takes your order or your money and you can't sit down to eat. I figure that's to get around the law, since he's not exactly selling anything, just making it available. What I don't understand is why Mama helps him break the law and the Sabbath for the sake of a jelly donut.

I guess church for Mr. O'Shea is 89.3 AM on the radio. When you walk in the Donut Hole on a Sunday, he's always singing along with the Florida Boys or the Gaither Trio, "I'll Fly Away" or some such ringing out over the sound of the sizzling grease in the big fryer.

"Mama," I said once when we got back to the car with our donuts. "Aren't we kind of sinning when we help Mr. O'Shea work on the Sabbath?" I didn't dare mention the part that we were also partners in crime. Daddy gave me a look in the rearview mirror like I had just grown three more ears or something, but it was too late. The question was already out there.

She jerked her head around and glared at me and said, "It was the Sabbath and the Lord healed them all."

I nodded like that certainly cleared the whole thing up, and she turned around satisfied. But for me, the whole issue just shot a hole in the fabric of all that I thought I knew.

That hole grew deeper, darker, and more unbridgeable when Rachel and Samuel Katz moved to Collins.

RACHEL KATZ

Miss Rachel Katz moved to Collins with her brother, Samuel, right before my eleventh birthday. Mama and I met her at the A&P grocery store about a week after she got moved in. I tried to be helpful when I heard her muttering to herself and I told her the Malt-o-Meal was on the next aisle over. She stared at me a minute, then laughed and said she was looking for matzo meal. That was a new one on me, and apparently nobody in the store had ever heard of it either. She and Mama got to talking and they seemed to hit it off. Miss Rachel said I should come over and visit her. She said she got lonely here and didn't have much company. Mama was quiet for a few minutes and then she said, "Well, I 'spect that'll be all right."

So the next Saturday after we cleaned the house like Mama was expecting a visit from the queen, I went on over. Miss Rachel lived at the end of Elm Street, and there was a big field beside her yard and a vacant lot across the street where the Daughtry house had burned down. The Daughtrys had moved out in the country instead of building back. On the other side of her house, in the big side yard, there was a garden with so many flowers, trees, and shrubs you couldn't even see the neighbors' house. If you didn't know better, you'd think she was all alone on a big plantation like Tara in *Gone with the Wind*.

I knocked on the door, and Miss Rachel called for me to come in. She was sitting in a pretty flowered arm chair with crocheted things over the back of it. She was reading her Bible and eating bread and honey.

"Come on in, Evangeline," she said. "You can help me celebrate the Sabbath." I felt bad for her because I figured she must have senile dementia. Mary Beth McClendon's grandmother had senile dementia and she thought she was married to Governor John Bell Williams. It happens when you get really old, like fifty, and Miss Rachel was at least that.

"Miss Rachel," I said real loud, "today is Saturday. Tomorrow is the Sabbath. Did you try to go to church today? Didn't you notice nobody was there?"

Miss Rachel just laughed. She had the nicest laugh. You couldn't help but smile, and want to laugh along with her. "Child, go over to that desk in the corner and bring me the calendar." I did. "Now look," she said. "What day is at the beginning of the week?"

"Sunday," I said.

"Now what day is the last, the seventh?"

"Saturday."

"What did God say in the scriptures?" She didn't give me time to answer. "He said in six days you shall do all your work, but the seventh . . . now, Evangeline, which day does that calendar say is the seventh?"

"Saturday, but . . ."

"But the seventh," she continued, "is a day of rest, a holy Sabbath for the Lord. In it you shall do no work."

She offered me some bread, she called it challah, and honey, and I said, "Yes, thank you," and sat down to wait for it, puzzling over this Sabbath thing. I knew Brother Browne and the people over at Crossroads Missionary Baptist Church would be mighty disappointed if it was true. They made a real big deal about Sunday being the Lord's Day.

After she set my plate down, along with a big glass of cold milk, she took her Bible and showed me the verse she was talking about.

100

"Oh," I said, "you're reading from the 'Old Testament.' You need to read the 'New Testament.' That's the one Jesus and the disciples read."

She coughed into her napkin, then smiled and said that what I called the 'New Testament' was written a number of years after Jesus died. "When Jesus and his disciples talked about the scriptures," she said, "they were talking about the law and the prophets, what you call the 'Old Testament.'"

Well, that was a bigger mouthful to chew than the bread I was munching, so I just sat quiet and thought about it. Nobody had ever told me that before and I never thought about it. We always studied the "New Testament" at church, the King James Version.

I went to see Miss Rachel a lot over the next few weeks, but we didn't talk about the Bible. She told me about her family in Germany and how most of her kin-folk had been killed during the war. She and her brother had been sent to America by some kind people in Hamburg and they grew up in New York with a cousin of their mother's. Her brother, Samuel, worked in manufacturing and became one of the big wheels there in New York. The reason they moved to Collins was so he could run the new factory in Mt. Olive. Samuel had married a girl in New York and Miss Rachel had lived with them and took care of their children, while Samuel's wife taught school. She never did get married herself. She wasn't fat or ugly, so I don't know why she didn't get a husband, but she didn't. Anyway, Samuel's children grew up and moved away and his wife died, so now it was just Miss Rachel and Mr. Samuel. He had to travel back and forth to New York all the time, so Miss Rachel was alone a lot.

One Saturday when I left Miss Rachel's, Tommy Garner and Joe Paul Greer were walking by right when I came out her front gate. I was headed for the Sinclair station to check the Coke machine for RC bottle caps because six bottle caps would get you into the afternoon matinee at the Rebel Theater. Joe Paul and

Tommy stopped me and Joe Paul said, "What you doing in there? You a Jew lover?"

"What are you talking about?" I said. "Get out of my way." I tried to shove past, but they blocked me.

"That old woman is a Jew," Joe Paul said.

"So?" I wasn't real sure what a Jew was, but the way Joe Paul said it I didn't think anybody as nice as Miss Rachel could be one.

"So," he said, stabbing his finger into my shoulder, "the Jews killed Jesus, and if you don't want to go to hell with them, you better quit spending time with Christ killers."

Tommy stood there nodding, but I don't think he knew what Joe Paul was talking about any more than I did.

"Well, Miss Rachel wasn't born when Jesus died, so even if she is a Jew, she didn't help kill him."

"Doesn't matter," Joe Paul said. "You can't love the Jews and love God, too. So you better stay away from there. They get what's coming to them, and so do Jew lovers."

"Yeah," echoed Tommy. "Jew lovers get what's coming to them."

"You're both ignorant," I said, although I wasn't certain. "You don't even go to church. What do you know about it?"

"I know what my old man told me and he knows for sure. His Uncle Jesse was a preacher over in Prentiss. Uncle Jesse said the Jews killed Jesus and because of that God chose the Baptists to be His new people and the Jews are going to hell."

Well, I had already heard the Catholics were doomed because of all that idol worship and stuff, but I didn't know about the Jews. I told Joe Paul it seemed like God was gonna run out of people pretty soon because I knew some Baptists that might not make the cut either. He said I was just a baby and didn't know anything about grown-up stuff. I pointed out that I was almost eleven and he was only thirteen, and I was a whole lot more grown up than he was most of the time. He pushed me into the fence and called me a titty baby, pretty much proving my point.

"Uncle Jesse said they had some Jews try to live in Prentiss one time, but they didn't stay long, and these Christ killers won't be here long either. You wait and see."

"Get out of my way," I said again, but Joe Paul crowded me up against the fence.

"Hey, her old man's coming," said Tommy and the boys ran off as Daddy walked to the fence.

"What was that about, Vangie?" Daddy asked. "Did those boys hurt you?"

"No, Daddy, but they called Miss Rachel . . . they called her a bad name."

"What bad name, Vangie?"

"They called her . . . a Jew," I whispered.

"Vangie, Jew isn't a bad name. It means a person from Israel and it's like saying Italian or Irish."

"Well, that shows what they know," I said. "Miss Rachel is from New York. Well she was born in Germany, so I guess she's German. Wait until I tell them."

"Now, hold on, Vangie, it means religion, too, like Baptist or Methodist. A person can be a Jew because of what they believe and because their family came from the Israelites."

"But the Israelites were good, weren't they? In Sunday school, Mrs. Cranford said God told Moses to get the Israelites out of Egypt 'cause they were His chosen people and then He parted the Red Sea and drowned all the Egyptians that were chasing after them."

"I don't know a whole lot of Bible teaching, Vangie. I just know hating people can't be what God's all about. Maybe you should go talk to the preacher."

Daddy always says if you want to know something, go straight to the horse's mouth, so Sunday after church I went to see Miss Rachel. She opened the door and asked me in and went straight to the kitchen, but I didn't think I could eat any bread right then. Miss Rachel looked so kind, and I couldn't imagine her in a devil's hell with flames licking at her for all eternity like Brother Browne said happened to people who reject our Lord and Savior, and like Joe Paul and Tommy said would happen to all the Jews. I started bawling my head off just thinking about it.

Miss Rachel put her arms around me, saying, "Shhh. Shhhh." When I could talk again, she made me tell her what was wrong and I told her what those boys had said. "You want to know something?" she said finally. "Jesus was a Jew. He was born in Israel and he went to synagogue—that's the Jewish church. So if those boys say they love Him, they're Jew lovers, too." Then she started laughing and so did I, even though I couldn't wait to tell Tommy and Joe Paul. I said I believed I could eat some bread and honey, and we finished our visit listening to some really pretty violin music on the hi-fi and talking about growing African violets.

I didn't think about any of that again until one night in October when I heard Daddy telling Mama that somebody had come up on Miss Katz's porch in the dead of night and had written "Christ Killer" on her front door in red paint.

"Daddy, I think I might know who did that," I said, coming into the living room.

"Evangeline," my Mama started in that voice that meant I'd be upstairs in my room in a minute, but Daddy asked who I thought would do something like that. I told him everything Tommy and Joe Paul had said and he nodded and said, "Greer. It figures. Don Greer is the biggest bigot I ever knew, and he's raising that boy to be the same way."

"Now, Joseph, little pitchers . . ." said Mama.

"Daddy, why do Joe Paul and his daddy hate Miss Rachel?" I interrupted. "Why do they hate Jews?"

"That's what I don't like about religion, Vangie," Daddy said. "It's full of hate."

"Joseph!" Mama cried. "How can you say that? The Good Lord isn't about hate."

"I didn't say anything about the Lord, Emily. I was talking about religion. They don't usually go together."

Now I was really confused. I spent some time thinking about what Mama, Daddy, and Miss Rachel said and decided maybe they were all right in some way, if you took God out of the church and the synagogue and just looked at Him plain.

I noticed that people in town were starting to act kind of funny. Even in church Brother Browne was talking more about separating ourselves from unbelievers than he was about how to become a believer, which was what he usually talked about every Sunday of the year, even though by now we all just about had to be believers. I, personally, thought it was about time we moved on to something else. I didn't dare say anything, though, because the one time I did, Mama pinched my ear until I thought she'd twist it right off in her hand.

One Friday about two weeks after the paint thing, me and Mama were at the A&P in Mount Olive and Miss Rachel came in. I was about to go say hey when Mrs. Carmichael and Mrs. Haverty came around the corner, stopped in front of Miss Rachel, then turned and walked the other way—right while Miss Rachel was trying to say good morning.

She turned red and looked down at the floor, and I ran over to her and started pushing her grocery buggy for her. She perked up and acted like nothing had happened, but every now and again I saw her lip kind of tremble. It made me mad as all get out to think of those ladies snubbing her like that, but Miss Rachel wouldn't talk about it.

I know some of the ladies had tried to get Mama to stop me from seeing Miss Rachel, but Mama never said a word to me about it. I was real proud of her, the same as when she didn't back down from letting Hettie Fairley stay with us last year. Hettie was an old colored woman who took in laundry to help take care of her three grandchildren who'd moved to Jackson with Hettie's daughter, May Ellen. Hettie's husband, Old George—that's what everybody called him—had got kicked in the head by a mule he was hooking up to a plow and died. They couldn't pay the rent on the little farm and Hettie didn't have any people close by and didn't have anywhere to go. Everybody said what a shame it was, but nobody made a move to help her, so Mama asked Daddy if she could stay with us until she could get enough money to go to Jackson and be with May Ellen. I thought it was great having Hettie live with us. She stayed in the spare room down the hall from me and she told the best stories, and boy could she make tea cakes. For a little while, the women snubbed Mama just like they had done Miss Rachel. I wasn't allowed to play with some of the girls from school, but after Hettie moved on, it seemed like everybody just kind of forgot about it.

But now here they were being mean to somebody else. I figured we'd be out of favor again because I knew Mama wouldn't be mean and I knew Daddy wouldn't be quiet.

One Friday night in late November, I headed over to Miss Rachel's to see if I could help her and Mr. Samuel get ready for Christmas. I had noticed they hadn't put up one single decoration. Miss Rachel didn't go out much anymore. A lot of the time she sent me to the store for her with a list and more money than I needed. She always told me to keep the change.

I timed it where I'd get to her house just as dusk was falling— that was right when the bread would be coming out of the oven, and I loved it when she opened the oven door and that fresh bread smell just filled up the house. Mr. Samuel was out of town again and I knew Miss Rachel would pour just the tiniest bit of wine in my grape juice. It made me feel grown-up, but I didn't dare tell anybody. Miss Rachel didn't know it, but at the Missionary Baptist Church we had a covenant hanging on the wall saying we wouldn't drink alcohol. I hadn't signed anything, so I didn't figure I was breaking any rules, but I didn't think Mama would see it that way.

We ate big bowls of beef stew with our bread and juice, and were sitting in the living room having apple cake, when we heard a noise outside. I started to get up, but Miss Rachel pushed me back down on the couch and turned toward the door with a real funny look on her face. Then I heard what she must have heard first. "Jews," somebody was saying. Then louder, "Go back up north and live with the niggers. We don't want your kind here."

Miss Rachel pursed her lips, then went and flung open the front door, not even noticing me right behind her. I saw some people run off into the bushes near the big field. "Cowards," she yelled, then turned to go back inside when somebody ran back and heaved a big brick toward the porch, then ran off again.

"Watch out," I yelled, but the brick hit Miss Rachel right in the top of the back of her head. She fell with a thump and blood started pooling around her like a bright red halo. I ran inside and called home. I was crying so hard that Daddy had to ask me three times what was wrong before I could make him understand that Miss Rachel was dying.

The ambulance and the police chief got to the house before Daddy did, and Chief Cole asked me what happened. I told him and I told him about Joe Paul and Tommy and what they had said. I'd heard grown-up people around town saying some of the same things lately. Joe Paul was trashy and ignorant, so maybe he couldn't be blamed so much, but I thought the grown-up people, especially the ones that were always having bake sales for some mission, ought to know better.

Joe Paul's family wasn't anywhere to be found by the time Chief Cole got around to looking them up. Some folks said they had family in Arkansas in the mountains and they might have gone there. Their Uncle Jesse in Prentiss swore that they had moved away before the night Miss Rachel was attacked, but I'd bet anything it was Joe Paul that threw that brick. I had got a glimpse of dark hair, blue jeans, and a red plaid shirt—just like Joe Paul wore most of the time. And it wasn't just kids out there that night.

It was too dark to see who they were, but there were grown men. The chief didn't listen to me. He just patted me on the head like an annoying puppy and talked over me.

For the next week, people stood around and whispered, and they'd always stop talking whenever they saw me. I went to the hospital every day. Miss Rachel wouldn't open her eyes when I stood by her bed and held her hand, and Mr. Samuel told me it would be best if I didn't come back. I did though. I didn't go in her room, but I went to the hospital every afternoon as soon as I got out of school and just sat in the chairs in the lobby. She didn't die, but when she got out of the hospital, Mr. Samuel put her in the car and drove away going back to New York. Miss Lela at Cavendish Realty put a sale sign in the front yard, but it was almost a year before anybody bought their house.

People around town would still stand in groups and talk about what a shame it was and how awful that anybody had so much hate in their hearts. They seemed to have forgotten that just a few weeks before, they had been muttering about Jews themselves. They didn't seem to realize their words and meanness had hurt Miss Rachel as much as that brick had. Maybe more.

I think now, as I often do, about the strength of character Rachel and Samuel Katz had and how deeply proud they were of their heritage.

Heritage was a big thing in my family as well, although I never recognized it as such while I was growing up. We had no social barriers or discrimination because of ethnicity or religious beliefs, but coming from a place called Sullivan's Hollow did raise some eyebrows among Mississippians who had heard the tales of the Hollow. Local folklore told of a tough Irish bunch that reigned in Smith and the surrounding counties. I grew up on stories of men who fought hard, lived tough, loved deep, and couldn't resist a practical joke any more than an active alcoholic can resist a bottle of bourbon. No, like the Katz family, we didn't hide our heritage. My family wore ancestry around like a mink coat, just waiting for an opportunity to brag about it.

THE MACRAES OF KINTAIL

I could hear Grandpa MacRae talking to my cousin Duncan. "Young Duncan, lad, ye've a verra fine heritage ta uphold," Grandpa said in his thick Scottish brogue. "And I want to tell ya a wee bit about those as came afore ya."

Both my grandfathers on my mother's side felt honor bound to keep family history alive. Granddaddy Sullivan's family was a colorful bunch who originated in County Cork, Ireland, descended from Donal Cam O'Sullivan through Sir Owen O'Sullivan of Dunboy Castle.

I liked hearing about that and would imagine myself as lady of the manor. I remember one time I started drinking hot tea in the mornings and calling my buttered biscuits scones. After the first morning or two of this, Aunt Lavinia just rolled her eyes and went back to praying as she often did in my company.

According to Granddaddy, there was fierce battle at Dunboy Castle against the British in the early 1600s, and the surviving Sullivan sons fled to America when the castle was vanquished. I could see brave young men, all with my cousins' faces, fighting valiantly before rushing to their boats to go to the New World. They settled in North Carolina then some spread out to Georgia. In the early 1800s a couple of brothers, Owen and Thomas, moved to Alabama. Owen stayed there, but his brother moved on to the fertile lands of Smith County, Mississippi, Granddaddy says. There, Thomas Jefferson Harvey Sullivan, "Pappy Tom," founded Sullivan's Hollow. The new Mississippi Sullivan castle was a log cabin that still stands proudly near Mize. I went there at

Thanksgiving a few times. It still has the old furniture in it, and I love looking at the pictures on the walls of Pappy Tom and his family

Anyway, Thomas Sullivan populated the Hollow with twenty-two little Sullivans, eleven courtesy of his first wife, Maud Elizabeth Arnold. When she died, probably worn out with child bearing, he married a woman named Mary Polly Workman, and fathered eleven more. I am an only child, but with all the cousins I have to deal with, I can imagine what kind of crazy it must have been with that many kids running around. But I guess they were good Christians because they certainly obeyed the commandment to be fruitful and multiply. Their fine fighting spirit was kept alive as well.

The exploits of the Sullivans of Sullivans Hollow—especially Wild Bill, the acknowledged "king of the Hollow"—are well known in Covington and Smith counties and are bandied about in some form all over Mississippi. Granddaddy Sullivan, as his forbears before him, made sure the family stories lived on intact by telling and retelling them to wide-eyed audiences of children, grandchildren, great-grandchildren, and various and sundry nieces and nephews. After he died, my uncles took up the mantle, ensuring that Sullivan history would survive as long as Sullivan DNA. I learned about DNA in biology this year at Collins High School.

I think Grandpa MacRae felt a little competitive with the Sullivan side since the Fighting MacRaes, as they were known, never actually owned a castle and nobody was named "Sir" anything. He made a big point of letting us all know that the MacRaes were the constables of Eilean Donan, the castle of Clan McKenzie in Dorney, Scotland near the Isle of Skye. Grandpa Mac had plenty of stories, but without the blue blood in his veins, he opted for authenticity by way of adopting a brogue and obtaining, Lord only knows where, a magnificent kilt. He only wore that once, though. Grandma Josie put her foot down when she saw him regally descending the stairs one Christmas morning in his finery. Authentic Scots forsook undergarments apparently.

I got in big trouble once when Grandpa Mac caught me wearing his kilt with one of Mama's old silk blouses. I figured if he wasn't going to be allowed to wear it, there was no sense in it just going to waste. Aunt Lavinia could make me a fine skirt out of it. When he saw me, his face turned all red and blotchy, and for a minute he lost his brogue along with his temper. "Evangeline Tanner!" he yelled, one of the few times I ever heard him raise his voice. "What in thunder do you think you're doing?"

"I thought if you weren't gonna wear it, I could make a skirt out of it," I said, my lip beginning to quiver. The first tear carried his temper away like a wave washing out a footprint. "Aw, lass," he said then, brogue and equanimity equally restored, "Tis not a piece of fabric. That kilt, in the MacKenzie tartan, is a bit of your history, a part of your blood and bone. It's respect for the MacRaes of old that made us who we are today."

I threw my arms around him, sobbing, his kindness and quick forgiveness undoing me more completely than his anger ever could have. He hugged me close and whispered, "I'll tell ye a secret. The minute your Grandma Josie leaves the house, the kilt comes out of the closet and I raise a glass to the spirits of MacRaes long gone and all that are yet to come."

Wide-eyed, I said, "Grandma lets you keep alcohol here?"

"Lets?" he said, indignant. "Nobody *lets* a MacRae do anything. We do as we wish."

I didn't mention the fact that he wasn't allowed to wear the kilt and had to sneak around to raise that glass. I silently agreed to ignore that discrepancy, and he silently agreed to ignore my disrespect to The Kilt.

Anyway, the MacRaes kept their own heritage alive just as obstinately as the Sullivans, going so far as to ensure there was a Duncan MacRae in every generation, named after the Duncan MacRae who was constable in the 1500s. It was to this most recent Duncan that Grandpa was endeavoring to impart familial pride, a difficult task, as no seven-year-old could possibly have cared any less about his fine heritage than did young Duncan MacRae. It didn't help matters that the closest Grandpa has ever been to Scotland is the Scotch tape aisle in the Ben Franklin store in Collins, Mississippi.

"Vangie, lass," he said as I came in the room. "Did I ever tell ye about the MacRaes of Kintail?" Of course, we both knew I heard those stories at least once a month, but I wouldn't hurt Grandpa's feelings for anything. Little Duncan took this distraction as an opportunity to defect to the dining room where my cousin Denver Reardon was relating a tale far more appealing to a little boy.

Denver was telling about the time Wild Bill Sullivan tied a dead corn snake to his brother Neece's foot while Neece was asleep by their camp fire. I had heard this story just as often as I'd heard about the MacKenzies and MacRaes. Apparently, after the reptile was secured to Neece's ankle, Bill fired his shotgun and yelled, "Snake." Neece jumped up, saw the snake by his foot and took off running and jumping, thinking the thing was chasing him. When he figured out what Bill had done, he came back to the fire and made Bill stay awake all the rest of the night—probably at gunpoint, Denver said—to pay for the joke.

I took Duncan's place at Grandpa's feet and drank in the sound of his voice along with the story of the scattered children of Kintail. I loved hearing the old stories and could hardly wait until I was old enough to go see Ireland and Scotland for myself.

Grandma Josie called Grandpa in to the kitchen just as Grandpa got to the part about the destruction of the MacKenzie castle, so I joined Duncan in the dining room to listen to Denver.

Denver was related to me through both sides of Mama's family. Apparently two MacRae brothers married Sullivan sisters and one of the resulting MacRae daughters married a Reardon, and voila, Denver. Denver embodied the heritage of both Sullivans and MacRaes. He was just as full of both fun and mischief, and I figure only stricter law enforcement of modern times kept him from pulling the same kinds of stunts as Wild Bill and Neece. I figure one day some little Bill Sullivan will be hearing tales of his great uncle Denver Reardon.

Thinking of Denver softens the hard edges of this day. Fairly early on in my life, he became my hero and mentor. Thinking of how he would handle situations helped me navigate some difficult passages in my life. I remember when my devotion began.

DENVER REARDON

I watched this movie where Loretta Young was a nun named Sister Margaret and she and Sister Scholastica—isn't that the most awful name?—came from France to start a hospital for children. I think Sister Margaret was *the* most amazing woman and I want to be an amazing woman like that. I am going into eighth grade in September, and it's time I figure out my future.

I used to want to be like Melanie in *Gone with the Wind*. She was sweet and selfless like Sister Margaret. But then I kind of wanted to be like Scarlett O'Hara, too. The only thing is Scarlett didn't know a thing about true love. That's why she married all those men that were wrong for her while Rhett Butler was right there all crazy in love with her.

When I was young, back in fifth and sixth grade, I had planned to get married and have children like Mama thought I should, but then some things happened that made me decide I never wanted to get married. I figured the best thing was to be a Bohemian artist. My aunt Tiny heard me telling my cousin Johnny Earl about wanting to be an artist and she said that was a sinful way to want to live. She said my mama was right and God intended for me to get married and raise babies.

Before I watched that movie, I had resigned myself to my fate, and planned on staying in my room in abject misery for the next few years until it was time to get married. Maybe do some sketching that would be discovered by my grandchildren.

But after I saw Sister Margaret, I started thinking about getting me to the nunnery. It would save me from marriage at least, even if I couldn't be a Bohemian artist. I didn't know where there were any Baptist convents, but I figured I better find one quick. I wasn't getting any younger.

Then Denver Reardon came riding in on his big white horse. Well really it was a Greyhound bus, but Denver was my knight in shining armor, even though he was my third cousin and way older than me, like in his twenties. I always liked to talk to Denver because he didn't treat me like a little kid. He really listened to what I said. He had come over with his parents to have dinner with us, and Mama let me out of doing dishes so I could visit with Denver. She said she and Aunt Ida Mae needed to catch up and they'd do dishes. Daddy was out in the barn with Denver's daddy.

"Denver," I said when we went out on the front porch swing after dinner, "sometimes I wish I was a man and could be a merchant marine like you or something."

"So why don't you?" he asked, pushing the swing back and forth with the toe of his boot.

"Be a man?" I asked, thinking he must have salt water on his brain.

"No, dummy, be a merchant marine or something."

"Well, I can't."

"Hunh," he said, stopping the swing and turning sideways to stare at me. "Oh, you poor thing. Born without a brain, were you?"

"No," I retorted. "I'm a girl."

"Oh." He just looked at me for the longest time. Then he poked at my right arm, said, "Hunh" again and stared some more. Just as I started to fidget, he said, "So, girls have to surrender their arms and legs at puberty, then."

I blushed because I knew what puberty was, but I'd never heard anybody mention it except for during "The Talk."

"No," I said.

"Eighteenth birthday?"

"No."

"Then, why can't a person, girl or not, with a brain, two arms, and at least one leg do whatever she wants?"

"But it isn't ladylike."

"According to who?" He started swinging again and took a toothpick out of his pocket and started chewing on it.

"Everybody."

"Since when have you met everybody?"

"Well, you know what I mean," I said, feeling a little confused.

"Yeah, I know what you mean." He was silent for a while and we just sat there swinging and listening to the frogs and crickets. "You know, Vangie," he said a little later, "when I was growing up everybody talked about me being a farmer. My daddy, and his daddy, and his, and all as far back as anybody can remember were all cattle farmers. But all I wanted was to go to sea. I used to build pretend boats and put them in the middle of the cow pasture and sit in them. In my mind I was riding the waves. When the cows passed by, I'd pretend they were whales. A whole pod of whales. Those white cow birds were sea gulls to me. I read everything I could about boats, ships, and sailors."

"What did your family say?" I asked.

"Well, when I first started talking about it, they did about the same thing they do to you. They laughed when I was little, then when it quit being funny, they started talking about what was proper and expected. Started talking about duty."

"So what did you say?"

"Nothing. I just quit talking about it. But I never quit dreaming about it, and I never quit planning. When I was eighteen, I was old enough to make my own decisions, and I packed my bags and went to New Orleans to try to get on with a river boat. Before that, I'd never been on anything bigger than my daddy's fishing boat on the Okatoma River."

My eyes felt as big as Mama's fine bone china collector's plate. "What did your daddy do to you?" I asked.

"Not a thing," he said. "Oh, he was mad for a while. Threatened to disown me. But the first time I came home, we had a sit down and he said he didn't understand why I wanted to be away from home and the farm, but he loved me and hoped I was happy."

Denver got quiet and started chewing on his toothpick again, and I started chewing on what he'd said. I remembered Daddy saying once that we can choose what we want to be, and now Denver was talking about choosing what you wanted over what everybody wanted for you. It was a lot to think about and I didn't know if I had the guts to be like Denver. He was a hero in my mind.

By accident or Divine Design, the next thing I feel in the box is a .45 bullet casing, which keeps my thoughts centered on Denver. He had so much influence on my life, and not all of it good, necessarily. I remember when I was fifteen and he came to stay with us until time to ship out again. His friend Canton Kindle came to visit. It was the day of the great shootout.

SHOOTOUT

Canton Kindle was very . . . present. He didn't walk, he strode through the house, every step rattling the knick knacks on the shelves. He didn't ring a doorbell; he jabbed at it four or five times, or banged on the door instead of just knocking. Often, he peered in the window and tapped on the glass at the same time. His version of tapping made us all cringe and wait for the broken glass to come flying. Somehow it never did.

Canton always came over when my favorite cousin, Denver, was at our house, and Denver always stayed with us whenever he wasn't at sea. He said if he stayed at home his mama would drag him off to church every time the doors opened and have the entire congregation lay hands on him. They went to a Pentecostal church and the doors opened a lot. I wasn't allowed to go to the Pentecostal church. I don't know if they were among the bunch that was going to hear the Lord say, "Depart, I never knew you," like the Catholics, but there was something about it that Mama hadn't approved of.

Anyway, whenever Canton came over, he'd say to Denver, "Let's go raise some eyebrows," and off they'd go to get up to some mischief or other. I was just a kid to them, so they never let me go with them, but I'd hear the grownups talking about whatever they had done. The women would mostly be wringing their hands and praying that the Good Lord would intervene and "deliver them from the power of darkness," but Daddy and the uncles would just laugh and shake their heads and call them "cards."

On this particular visit, though, I thought even the menfolk might do a little hand wringing. Uncle Calvin and Aunt Lavinia had gone to Hot Coffee for the weekend. They took Cletus with them after he said he was going to get the shotgun and stake out the perimeter. Then early in the morning, Daddy had gone over to Grandpa MacRae's to help him on the farm. He said I could stay home with Denver. After all, Denver was twenty-two, and I was fifteen and practically a grown woman myself. My great-grandmother MacRae was married and had two babies by the time she was my age.

Canton came over right after lunch and told me he and Denver had man stuff to talk about and I was to stay out of the living room. He had a jacket draped over his arm, but I could tell he was using it to cover up something in his hand. When they had time to get settled, I pushed the door open a crack and peeked in. Canton was taking a cork out of a big brown jug. He sniffed the jug, made a face, lifted it, and took a big swig, then passed the jug to Denver. Well, I knew what was in that jug. I'm no baby and I've heard of moonshine. But I figured it was no skin off my nose, so I went outside to see if Rusty, the old horse that Daddy bought to keep from mowing the pasture, was in the mood to let me ride. He wasn't, but I rode him anyway. After I got him galloping up and down the big field a few times, his manners improved a whole lot.

When I got done riding, I turned Rusty back out in the pasture and went for a walk in the woods and sat down by the stream a while. When I went back to the house, I heard the television blaring at top volume. A Western, I figured, with all the shooting that was going on. I opened the door a little and saw the brown moonshine jug laying on the floor by the chintz sofa Mama saved up for and bought just before my thirteenth birthday. Canton and Denver had Daddy's matched set of Colt .45 Peacemakers. Canton was wearing the holster. Both of them were standing up, wobbling a bit, and staring at the screen. "Watch it," Canton shouted, slurring noticeably, and aimed the gun at the television and pretended to shoot. "Got 'im," he said. "Before old Bat Mashterson even got hish gun drawn."

"You're fash. Yes shiree," Denver agreed. "But jush wait." He pulled the other .45 out of his pants pocket, aimed, said bang, then blew on the barrel. "I got that one."

I stood frozen in the door way, afraid to do anything that might cause one of them to get too excited. They were pretty well lit and I had seen Edgar and Alva Atmore first hand and knew what could happen when a person got all liquored up.

I was looking for an opportunity to step in and maybe get the pistols or at least distract the boys, but it was all going too fast. First Denver then Canton would spot a bad guy—although sometimes it turned out to just be a cactus—and would aim the gun and yell bang. I was pretty worried because that Zenith twenty-three-inch console they were aiming at was Daddy's pride and joy.

He'd had to fight hard to get it, back when I was in second grade or so. Mama had said it was a doorway to the devil's workshop and she wasn't having any part of it. The radio was bad enough, according to her, but the worst thing that had ever come from that as far as I could see was Daddy could tune in Cuba on Sunday nights. It may have been the devil on there, but he was speaking Cuban so we never knew what he said.

I wanted a color television after Mary Beth McClendon got one the beginning of seventh grade and invited me over to her house to watch "Star Trek." But Mama had put her foot down and said there was no way any child of hers was going to go blind from watching that sin box in her own home. She had heard all about the evils of television, and color television was particularly bad as it damaged you physically as well as spiritually. I didn't see where "Bonanza" or "Roy Rogers" was all that sinful, and I didn't dare tell her I could see just fine even though I had been watching color television every week at Mary Beth's. And I sure wasn't going to mention the fact that Mama regularly watched "Lawrence Welk" and "Ted Mack's Amateur Hour." Of course, it wasn't in color. But like I said, Daddy loved that old console. I think mainly it was a reminder of the one time he had won an argument with Mama.

Anyway, I was trying to figure out something I could do to make them put the guns down long enough for me to grab them and run, when the stage coach on the show was ambushed by a gang of robbers that came swarming down out of the hills. Canton and Denver went into a frenzy then. I never knew which one of them it was that actually pulled the trigger, but there was a huge boom and the twenty-three-inch was blown to smithereens. Before we could react to that, it burst into flames.

"Damn!" I said, then clapped my hand over my mouth, more horrified by what I had said than by the sight of the pitiful, burning corpse of Daddy's Zenith.

Canton holstered his revolver, shook his head a couple of times, then yelled, "Geshsum water."

Denver just stared at him. He slapped at the side of his own head, then yelled, equally loud, "What'd you say? Whose father?"

My own ears were ringing pretty loud, so I figured both of them were stone deaf.

"Hey," Denver yelled, "We better put that out." He grabbed a cushion off the couch and began to beat at the flames with it.

"Mama's chintz," I cried, but neither of them heard me. Instead, Canton grabbed another cushion and soon they had smothered the flames. Very carefully they replaced the cushions, then stepped back, looking proud of themselves. To be fair, I guess maybe they had saved the house from burning.

I was standing there looking at the charred spots smeared over what had once been cheerful pink and blue flowers, when Canton leaned close to Denver and yelled into his ear, "You think old Rushty would let us shoot off hish back?"

I was momentarily relieved when Denver yelled back, "What are you thinking?" But then he added, "We have to reload first."

I'll never forget the look on Daddy's face when he came in and saw the destruction. And I learned later that it was a good thing that Denver and Canton were as drunk as they were when Rusty reared up, dumped them off, and fell back right on top of them after they both sent off a volley of shots at the big hay bale in the pasture. If they hadn't been limp as a bag of feathers, they probably would have broken half the bones in their bodies.

At least we did get a color television after that—and a new sofa.

As I tuck the casing back in the box, I see the cover of the manual from when I took Driver's Ed in the tenth grade. I suppose I put it in there to remind me of the momentous occasion of obtaining my driver's license, that passport to freedom that is one of the most revered rites of passage of the American teenager. Instead, it brings to my mind Daddy teaching me to drive his beloved Bel Air. Thought progression takes me to a particular trip in the Bel Air, but I wasn't driving. No, this was a hair-raising, eye-opening tool down the road with my daddy's sisters.

RIDING IN CARS WITH AUNTS

"Evangeline, you want to go shopping?" Aunt Tiny called. "I'm taking Helen downtown Collins to look for clothes."

Look was a relative term, as Aunt Helen is blind as a boulder. Given that, I figured this could be an interesting diversion and I needed a diversion badly. We had come to Uncle Brantley and Aunt Tiny's because Daddy had to pick up a cow nearby and he said I could visit with the cousins. But when we got here, Uncle Brantley and my cousins were all gone to the state fair up in Jackson. Not only that, Uncle Jules and Aunt Helen were here visiting and Uncle Jules sucks his teeth and talks non-stop about horticulture. I was so bug-eyed bored, I had almost gotten interested in the care and feeding of hybrid tea roses. As I said, I needed a diversion.

Five minutes later, I had my sweater in my hand and my new penny loafers on my feet and was standing on the front porch waiting for the aunts.

"Are you driving . . ." Aunt Helen walked onto the front porch, leaving Aunt Tiny behind. ". . . Brantley's truck?" she continued as Aunt Tiny stepped out.

"Well, of course I'm driving. Evangeline is only fifteen and you're blind."

"And you're deaf," retorted Aunt Helen. Then louder, she added, "I asked if you're driving Brantley's truck. 'Cause it makes my sciatica act up."

"I know that, Helen. I'm taking Joseph's Chevy. He took the truck and trailer to pick up that heifer, and Brantley took my car

129

to Jackson because Caroline says she wouldn't be caught dead in Joseph's car. Like she needs to impress somebody. Lord! That girl. I swanee! There's no living with her since she got that job at the Belk Whitney."

Aunt Helen had made her way down the steps and was headed across the yard toward the barn. Aunt Tiny grabbed her arm and turned her around. "Wrong way, Helen. Wait here with Vangie while I get the car." She strode off across the front yard, her turquoise blue flouncy skirt swinging from wide hips. Aunt Helen said, "So, Vangie, what grade are you in now?" She had asked me that at Christmas, just weeks ago, but maybe she hadn't realized it was me.

"Tenth," I answered, stepping around to face her.

"Collins High School?"

"Yes, ma'am."

"Keeping your grades up?"

"All As."

"That's good," she said. "If you can't get a husband, you can always make a teacher if your grades are good."

"Yes, ma'am," I said again, gritting my teeth. I was really tired of everybody assuming that my only choice in life was to get married and have a passel of children, but at the same time I was a little miffed that she seemed to think I might have trouble getting anybody to marry me.

Aunt Tiny drove up in the blue-and-white 1956 Chevrolet Bel Aire Daddy had bought after the wreck.

The Wreck. That seemed to be the line of demarcation in my life. Before the wreck, I had Mama; I hadn't become a woman yet; Aunt Lavinia didn't run the house; and I thought life would go on pretty much the same forever. A.W., After Wreck, I had a lot more freedom, but it had come at a horrible price. I found I had become a little rebellious, what with all that time to think for myself without Mama telling me I was wrong headed whenever I expressed a difference of opinion. Aunt Lavinia kept wanting to take me to the preacher to get me straightened out, but Daddy told her to let me be. Good thing we were Baptist; otherwise, I might have been in for an exorcism.

"Quit dawdling, girl, and help Helen get in the car." Aunt Tiny's deep bawling voice reverberated from a tall, stout form that belied the name she was given when she was a deceptively small infant. I took Aunt Helen's arm, but she shook it off. "Just walk in front of me," she said. "I can manage. I declare Tiny thinks I'm an invalid."

"I got the door, Aunt Helen," I said when we reached the car. I opened it and moved aside. "You can get in now." She slid into the front passenger seat, swinging her polyester encased legs carefully into the car, and I got into the back seat right behind her and sat looking at the back of her head. Aunt Helen was a skinny, spry little woman with black frizzy hair that came down just below her ears. She insisted on fixing it herself and wore it parted down the middle and slathered with VO5 Hair dressing to make it lay flat. She stopped short with the hair dressing cream though and the bottom poofed out suddenly, making her look like she was perpetually wearing ear muffs.

Helen, Tiny, and Lavinia were Daddy's sisters and I spent a lot of time in their company. They were about as different from Mama as a person could be and still be the same species. Still, I loved them, even though they did get on my nerves sometimes. To be fair, I probably wasn't exactly a picnic for them either.

We pulled out of the drive onto the gravel road that led to Highway 35, which would take us to Mount Olive, where we would take U.S. Highway 49 to Collins. "Lord it's warm for January," said Aunt Helen. "Y'all want 250 air conditioning or 450?"

"Four-fifty," I answered and we rolled down all four windows as the car picked up speed to fifty mph. As Aunt Tiny accelerated, I heard an odd scratching sound coming from overhead. After a minute, it stopped and I forgot about it as I stretched out in the back seat and got comfortable. The seats were a greenish blue vinyl and almost as long as the couch in our living room. Daddy loved that car. We'd go out driving on Sunday afternoons and sometimes he'd stop at the Burger Top and let me get a chili burger and a chocolate milkshake. I was a little surprised he let Aunt Tiny drive it, but I guess he had no choice since he took their truck.

Aunt Tiny drove with fierce concentration, leaning forward with her hands clenched on the steering wheel in a strict ten-and-two position. She wore leather driving gloves, which always looked out of place with her full skirts and ruffly blouses. As she carried at least seventy-five extra pounds, I thought she'd do herself a service if she wore polyester pants suits like Aunt Helen instead of all that yardage. Aunt Tiny, however, liked to say a woman was supposed to dress like a woman, not a man. She'd usually stare at Aunt Helen when she said it, but since Aunt Helen couldn't see her, it really didn't make any difference.

I had brought *Pride and Prejudice*, and settled down to read it until I heard Aunt Helen say, "Turn here."

"What?" Aunt Tiny asked.

"You missed your turn," Aunt Helen shouted.

"I haven't gotten to my turn, Helen. What are you talking about?"

"Wasn't that the road to 35?"

"No, that was the lumber mill."

"Well, don't miss your turn," Aunt Helen said. "You always pass your turn and then we have to go back."

"I do not," answered Aunt Tiny.

"You did last time," mumbled Aunt Helen.

"It's 10:15," said Aunt Tiny.

"What are you, the town crier?" asked Aunt Helen.

"What! You asked the time."

"I did not."

"You did, too. I heard you loud and clear."

"The last time you heard anything loud and clear was 1959."
Aunt Helen had her face toward the window.

"No, fifteen, not fifty-nine," said Aunt Tiny. "If you ask a
question, at least listen to the answer." In her aggravation, she
pressed harder on the gas pedal for a moment, lurching the car
forward before she let back off the gas. The scratching I'd heard
earlier returned louder and faster. "Did you hear that?" I asked.

"I didn't hear a thing," said Aunt Tiny.

"Now, that's the truth," said Aunt Helen, but so softly that
Aunt Tiny didn't catch it.

We rode on in silence for a while, with Aunt Tiny slowing
down as her irritation faded. "Where do you want to go first,
Helen?" asked aunt Tiny.

"Butler's, I guess. I need some new shoes. These are all
scuffed up."

How in the world she even knew what color they were much
less if they were scuffed, was beyond me. I hunched over the seat
and craned my neck to see the floorboard. Sure enough, the black
lace-up SAS shoes were showing some wear and tear.

"They're having a sale at Shainberg's," said Aunt Tiny.

"You missed it," yelled Aunt Helen.

"It just started today, Helen."

"No, you missed your turn. Again." A small, faintly smug
smile lifted her lip.

Aunt Tiny stared out the window. "Well. So I did," she said,
pulling into Schroeder's Fruit Stand right in front of an oncoming
truck, and turning the car around.

"How in the world . . ."

"What the hell is that?" asked Aunt Helen.

"What?" said Aunt Tiny.

"That noise."

"I don't hear anything," said Aunt Tiny.

"I do," I piped in from the back seat. "It sounds like scratching
on top of the car. I've heard it for a while."

"Watch that car," shouted Aunt Helen.

"Helen, you're blind as a bat," said Aunt Tiny. "Just hush and let me drive."

A loud horn sounded several times at that moment.

"I told you," said Aunt Helen.

"I was nowhere near it," said Aunt Tiny. "I don't know why they were blowing their horn."

Another car passed, and again honked as it went by, the driver pointing and gesturing toward our car. Aunt Tiny smiled and waved, and asked Aunt Helen what kind of shoes she wanted.

"Old Maine Walkers, and what was all that about?"

"Just friendly, I guess," said Aunt Tiny.

The scratching started up again as we rounded the curve that took us to Highway 49. It sounded like we were driving under small low-lying branches.

"There. That," said Helen.

"Nobody has hats anymore," said Tiny.

"Not hats. That. That infernal scratching," yelled Aunt Helen.

"Well, don't scream at me," said Aunt Tiny, swerving wildly as she turned in the seat to face her sister.

"I won't be screaming long. Because you're gonna get us all the hell killed."

Now, I wanted to scream.

"Watch the road," yelled Helen, as an eighteen-wheeler came from the opposite direction.

"I'm watching. I'm the one who can see, remember?"

I felt a sudden rekindling of interest in religion and closed my eyes to pray. I didn't re-open them until Aunt Tiny pulled off Highway 49 and crept down Main Street in Collins. A bit of scratching resumed momentarily and then all was quiet.

"Park here," barked Helen.

"For the love of heaven, Helen, this is the Texaco." A few moments later, she pulled into a space in front of Butler's. My renewed faith vindicated, I took a moment to thank God and opened my door.

When I got out, I stood staring at the top of the car. Aunt Tiny got out, followed my gaze, and muttered, "Well I never." Coriander, Aunt Helen's tortoise shell cat was standing stiff legged on the roof, hunched up, hair on end, with claw marks stretching out around her. She had somehow managed to snag her claws into something on the left side and had apparently been scrambling for purchase with her right feet, hanging on precariously the whole way to Collins. I was glad Aunt Tiny wasn't a speed demon, or Coriander would be nothing but a wet spot on the road.

Aunt Tiny stared at the cat, which was apparently frozen in fright looking for all the world like the Halloween black cat silhouettes, and Aunt Helen fumbled around for the door latch, yelling for somebody to let her out of the "damn car."

At that moment, I spotted Daddy coming down Main Street pulling the cattle trailer behind him. Certain now that there was a God, I flagged Daddy down, sprinted around the car, yanked Coriander off the roof, said I'd had enough shopping for one day, and hopped into the front seat of the truck. I put the still stiff Coriander on the floor board and swore to myself I would never get into a vehicle with my deaf and blind aunts again.

Daddy never said a word as he put the truck in gear. He didn't seem to find it at all odd that his daughter and a semi-catatonic cat had just jumped into the cab of his truck in the middle of downtown Collins. I can only assume he had ridden with the aunts before.

I prop myself against the headboard, arranging the pillows behind my back. Looking up, I watch the motion of the blades of the ceiling fan and think of Daddy, his sisters, and that old Chevy.

The Bel Air transported me to a night I will never forget. I have no memento in the box, but the sounds, sights, and feelings of that evening invade my mind as pervasively as the Kudzu vine on the hillsides lining the road. I was almost seventeen and, finally, Daddy had conceded that I should be allowed to date. I had waited what seemed like forever to my young mind, and there was a boy in school who was just as anxious. Gene Matheny had been asking me out since tenth grade. Even though I knew he was seeing Maggie Talbot at the same time, I daydreamed about the date we would one day have. How he would pick me up at the door, leaving Maggie behind forever, and escort me to his 1965 Mustang. When the date finally came to pass, Gene had banged up his Mustang taking a curve too fast. After a lot of begging, Daddy said I could use the Bel Air. I would be picking up my date instead.

FIRST DATE

I had pulled out everything in my closet, but there was never any real question. About the only things I had that weren't homemade were the orange and blue striped hip-hugger bell bottoms and sleeveless orange body suit I had bought with money saved up from Christmas and birthdays. I had found a pair of blue clip-on earrings in Mama's jewelry box and I put on my charm bracelet. A dab or two of Aunt Lavinia's Avon Cotillion, the only perfume in the house, and I was ready. It was the night of my long-awaited first date. I had had a boyfriend of sorts since first grade, but had become a born-again, dyed-in-the-wool romantic when I read *Wuthering Heights*. I had wanted to be desperately in love ever since, but not being able to even invite a boy over put a big crimp in that. Daddy said the rule was no dating until I turned seventeen. It was still two weeks before my birthday, but I had managed to convince Daddy that fourteen days would not make a difference.

Gene Matheny had been writing me notes since the beginning of tenth grade. He looked a lot like David Cassidy and all the girls were wild about him, especially Maggie Talbot. He was a senior and I was in eleventh grade, and he had asked me out to the movies a few times. I had to keep saying no, but I did dance with him at homecoming. Daddy dropped me off and picked me up, but at least I got to go. I think Aunt Lavinia convinced him. I think maybe she could see I was about ready to run off with Robby Mumford just to be able to see a boy, even though I didn't really want Robby to be my boyfriend.

Then one time I sneaked out. Gene asked me to go to prom with him and I knew if I said no he'd take Maggie Talbot. So Mary Beth McClendon and I made a plan. I went to spend the night with Mary Beth, and she loaned me her last year's prom dress to wear. I went to the prom with Mary Beth and her date, Gary Holifield. I didn't really count it as a date, but I did get to dance with Gene and before I left, he gave me his initial ring. He wanted to go out on a "going steady" date to make it official, but I didn't feel good about sneaking out and didn't want to do it again. Instead, I worked even harder at talking Daddy into letting me go out with Gene.

It took me two months, but Daddy finally said I could date; I took it as a great victory event though it was only two weeks until my birthday June 16th.

But this was it. The Night. The First Date. I thanked God for the mercy He had shown in having Daddy's Gun Club meeting rescheduled for tonight. Daddy had gone off with Thomas Wilkins, sparing me any additional lectures on proper behavior on my impending First Date. Aunt Lavinia tried to step up to the plate and prepare me for the pitfalls of going out with a boy, but I brushed past her, saying I had to hurry or Gene and I would be late. What we would be late for I didn't know, as Gene hadn't told me what he had planned; I just loved saying Gene and I.

"Gene and I; Vangie and Gene," I whispered. It felt so rich on my tongue, it almost had a taste. I was a couple. I had a boyfriend. I could date. All Aunt Lavinia had time to do was ensure that I had a dime for a payphone in case things went wrong. I didn't bother to remind her that I was the one with the car; I just blew past her, out the door, and down the steps, running headlong into adulthood.

I made myself drive carefully, pondering the protocol for picking up a boy for a date. Should I blow the horn? Ring the doorbell and escort him to the car? Neither felt right, but Gene saved me from the dilemma by waiting on his front porch. When

I drove up, he came down the walk and got in the passenger side. I was a little disappointed, as I knew Rock Hudson would have helped Doris Day out of the car, walked her around and opened her door. He would then take his place behind the wheel, all tall and manly. Gene just took some Juicy Fruit gum out of his shirt pocket and opened a stick, rolled it up, and popped it into his mouth, without even offering me a piece.

"Let's go to the Star," Gene said, chewing with his mouth open so the gum popped.

"That's all the way in Mendenhall, Gene."

"I know, but *The Godfather* is playing and I want to see it. Gene rolled down his window and let the warm summer air blow through his thick auburn hair. My own window was only open a crack, as I had spent twenty minutes curling my long straight brown locks and any hint of a breeze would straighten it as flat as if I'd ironed it.

"My Daddy would skin me alive if I went to see *The Godfather*," I said.

"Not *The Godfather*," Gene said quickly. "That's in Hattiesburg. I meant *Jeremiah Johnson*. That's at the Star."

"I don't know," I said. "Daddy didn't say I could leave Collins." I risked removing one hand from the ten-and-two position on the steering wheel to chew my fingernail. I didn't want to disobey Daddy, but I couldn't endanger my relationship with Gene. "Gene and I," I whispered to myself very softly.

"He didn't say you couldn't, did he?"

"Well, no," I answered.

"There you go," Gene said, satisfied. "You aren't breaking any rules. And besides, you're going to be seventeen next week, Vangie. You're practically a grown woman. You should be able to make your own decisions."

"In two weeks," I corrected automatically, still hesitant until Gene put one hand on my shoulder and said, "That's one of the things I love about you, Vangie. You're a strong woman."

The words mixed with the heady smell of his liberally applied English Leather cologne and I caved. Turning the car onto Hwy 49 North toward Mendenhall, I said, "Are we going to have time to get dinner, Gene?" Robert Redford would surely have taken his date out to dinner, probably to a high-class French restaurant with candles and wine.

"Yeah, sure," Gene answered, snapping his gum a record three pops in a row. "We can grab a burger."

A burger? This was nothing like I had pictured for my first real date, but I quickly regrouped. I didn't mind a burger. After all, Gene didn't make a lot of money working at the Texaco.

Gene turned on the radio, changing the station from Daddy's country AM station to WKNO and started singing along with Three Dog Night.

"Joy to the World. All the boys and girls. Joy to the fishes in the deep blue sea. Joy to you and me."

He punctuated his singing by jabbing me in the arm when he sang "you and me."

"Watch out," I said. The jab had made me jerk the wheel a bit.

"You're not a scaredy cat, are you?" he said, grabbing the wheel, causing the car to swerve violently.

"Cut it out, Gene," I said, feeling like my stomach had traded places with my tonsils.

Gene just laughed and turned the radio up.

I was beginning to consider going back home, when Gene walked his fingers up my arm and said, "You aren't mad are you, Babe?"

Babe. I was somebody's babe. I melted at the thought. "No, I'm not mad. It just scared me a little."

"Good."

We rode in silence for a while, the butterflies in my stomach, which had returned to its original position, fluttering all around the softly crooned word, "babe."

"Turn left up there," Gene said, scattering the butterflies along with my thoughts. "Next road. The Star is right there on Main."

Moments later, I pulled the car to a stop in front of the darkened theater, its marquis proclaiming "closed." When I turned to Gene, I thought for a moment I saw a peculiar little smile on his face.

"Rats," he said. "I forgot. Old man French closed it last year. Maybe I was thinking of Magee. Too late now."

"I guess we better head back to Collins," I said.

"No, let's go park at Legion Lake."

Legion Lake, I thought, confused. *It's dark. We can't fish, and we can't see to walk. Although the moon is pretty bright.*

"Park the car? Why?" I asked.

"You know," he said, "park." He gently squeezed my upper arm as he said it.

Park. For a moment I couldn't even remember the definition of park. Was it was a foreign word? Then conversations I had overheard in gym class began to play in my head. Angie Mosely started parking when we were in seventh grade. She was the only one who had grown boobs over the summer and all the boys at Collins Junior High, even the ninth graders, were asking her to go out with them. Angie's mother worked at the Red Rooster, a beer joint on Hwy 49 near Hattiesburg, and her daddy had gone to a sales convention two years ago and just never came back. Angie did whatever she wanted to, because her mother was asleep most of the day, then left for work at six every night. We were friends for a while, but then she said I was just a little girl and she had new friends now. I didn't care—she wasn't any fun anymore. I wondered if the boobs caused a personality disorder.

Anyway, I had heard what she and some other girls did when they "parked" with boys, and I wasn't having any part of that. Still, if I said no, he might take back his ring and our love affair would be over. My head warred with my heart, but I said, "No, we better go home, Gene. My Daddy would kill me if I went parking. He just now let me date."

Gene snorted. "Listen, Vangie, you're practically a woman. You're almost old enough to get married."

That didn't help his case any. Getting married was the last thing I wanted to do. I had been planning my career since I was eight. I still hadn't decided on which it would be, but it sure wasn't a housewife.

I had turned the car off when we stopped at the Star, and I reached now for the key to crank it. Gene put his hand over mine and said, "It's just that I've wanted to be alone with you for so long. Have you ever seen the lake under a full moon?"

I shook my head and let Gene take my hand. "I just want to show it to you. It's special and I want to share it with you because you're special, Vangie."

"I am?" I said breathily.

"Yeah, Baby. I want to share it with you, okay?"

I was overcome with pure unadulterated romance. My last holdout was shattered when Gene said, "Let me drive, Vangie. You shouldn't be having to drive on our first date." He was Rock Husdon, Robert Redford, David Cassidy. He had even swallowed his gum at some point and wasn't irritating me anymore. I remembered Mary Beth telling me that Gary took her parking at Lake Mike Connor once, and all they did was kiss. That wouldn't hurt anything. I wanted to be kissed. I said okay, and Gene got out and came around. He opened the door, but when I got out, he just hopped into the driver's seat instead of walking me around to the other side. I pushed down my annoyance, and got in the passenger side and Gene started the ignition and pulled away from the curb, almost hitting a black pickup that looked a lot like Mr. Wilkins' truck. When we got to Legion Lake, Gene parked near the dam. When he slid across the seat toward me, I quickly opened the door and got out. "You're right, Gene," I said. "Look at that lake."

Gene got out of the car, too, frowning. Then he looked up at the sky and smiled, pointing. "Look, there's the big dipper." It wasn't, but I stared at the night sky anyway and said, "Isn't it beautiful?" Gene moved closer, and this time I stayed still. There was a light breeze, and the fireflies were out, winking on and off, making the night as perfect as if God had created it especially for me. Gene put his arm around my waist and I snuggled against him.

When he turned to kiss me, I tilted my face slightly, the way I had practiced with the mirror. My first kiss, with J.R. in the band hall when I was twelve, was awful. We had bumped noses, then his glasses fell off. When our lips finally met, it felt like kissing the puckered end of a navel orange. I didn't see the attraction in kissing for a long time after that, although all the books made it seem so sweet. I kissed Jamie Albritton at a basketball game in ninth grade and it was a whole lot better. It was a little slobbery, but it at least made me want to try it again. But not with him. I found out he was holding hands with Carrie Anne Hennington under his jacket at the same time he was holding hands with me. She was sitting on the other side of him on the bleacher.

For a while, I met Robby Mumford at the public library in Collins. It was the only place we could meet because Daddy wouldn't give in and let me date no matter how hard I begged. My rationale of "all the other girls my age can date" fell on ears that might as well have been made of corncobs. Daddy wouldn't budge. So Robby and I met at the library. Daddy knew I loved the library and he never questioned me no matter how often I went or how long I stayed. I would check out a book, then meet Robby on the side of the building by the fountain. That way people coming down Main Street wouldn't see me and report back to Daddy. Robby was just a friend, but we both needed the practice.

My practice paid off, and apparently Gene had practiced, too, because my first kiss with him was worthy of any of the books I had read. I tried to cut my eyes around to see if my foot came off the ground like in the movies, but after a second I didn't care about my foot. The only body part I was aware of was my mouth—until Gene's hand began to move around from my back. As he inched closer to my breasts, I pulled away. "No, Gene," I said firmly. "We can only kiss."

He moved his hand back, and resumed the kissing. I was almost unaware of what his hands were doing until they started to unbutton my orange body shirt. "No," I said again. "I love you, Vangie," he said then. "Don't you love me?"

"I . . . ." I hesitated. Did I love him? I wanted to. My stomach was fluttering and my heart was hammering. That must be love. "I think I do," I whispered.

"Then show me. And let me show you how much I love you," he whispered, manipulating the second button open.

I swear, I heard my mother just then. "Vangie, don't make yourself cheap," she was saying, just like she did in my bedroom that day she explained the facts of life. "If a man loves you, he'll respect you. Promise me right now you'll wait until you're married before you . . ." Mama had trouble finishing the sentence. Finally, sweat glistening on her forehead, she whispered, "Before you . . . sleep with a man."

Like a dive into the icy water at Pep's Point near Hattiesburg, the memory effectively cooled my passion. Gene's, however, was still near the boiling point. I grabbed his hands, then pushed away.

"No. Not like this, Gene. I made a promise. I won't give myself to anybody but my husband."

"Then let's get married," he said, his breath coming in short, fast gasps. "Yeah, Vangie, we could go to Alabama and get married." Gene tried to pull his hands out of my grasp. "I heard there was a judge over there that would marry kids without their parents' consent. Remember George Matthews and Sandy Grayson? That's where they got married."

I remembered. And my cousin Otis had married Beverly Ann Burkhalter in Alabama a few years earlier. My sense of romance shifted into high gear. An elopement. I didn't want to be married, but I had dreamed of eloping for years. I felt like the same star struck kid I had been when I was thirteen and heard about Otis and Beverly Ann. Still . . . "I don't know, Gene," I said, still holding both his hands.

"I love you, Vangie. You're the most amazing girl. I want to be with you forever."

I was weakening. Then he said, "Prove you love me, then we'll head straight for Alabama." It was like another dip in that icy water. "Prove . . ." My indignant reply was smothered when Gene lunged forward, pulling his hands from mine, and covered my mouth with his own. His hands made up for lost time, too, and I was fighting to pull away when I heard a sound in the gloom on the other side of the dam. Gene was so overcome with either love or testosterone, he apparently didn't hear a thing.

"How 'bout *I* show you, son?" My daddy stepped out of the shadows, the bright moonlight gleaming off the Mossberg pump-action 12-gauge in his hands. He strode across the ground that separated him from us. "Want me to prove just how much I love you, boy?"

"No, no, s-s-s-sir," Gene stammered, backing away from me.

"Daddy, don't kill him," I screamed, as Daddy racked a double ought buck into the Mossberg. At the sound, Gene froze, nothing moving at all except for his eyes that grew impossibly large and the wet spot that appeared and began to spread across the front of his faded blue jeans.

"Come on," Daddy said, a big grin splitting his face. "I just want to show the boy some love."

Gene's paralysis was miraculously cured and he took off running toward the dam without a backward glance at me.

Daddy leaned the gun against the Bel Air and turned to me. My head dropped and tears of shame and fear began to roll down my cheeks. I felt his rough, calloused hand under my chin, gently lifting.

"What was going on in your head, Vangie?" he asked then. "Coming out here with a boy?"

"I didn't plan to, Daddy," I said through my sobs. "We were going to the movie. Gene said he wanted to go to the Star, but it was closed."

Something clicked in my mind. "Daddy, was that you and Mr. Wilkins we nearly hit when we left the Star?"

"It was Tom," Daddy answered. "He had gone to get some root beer and black walnut ice cream. When he saw the Bel Air, he thought it might be mine, so he came straight back and told me. I borrowed his truck and went to the Star, but y'all were gone, of course."

"How did you know to come here, Daddy?" I asked. I wondered if there was some sort of Daddy radar or telepathy that God installed for times like this.

"I was an eighteen-year-old boy once, Vangie," was all Daddy would say.

"Well, I'm glad you came when you did. I don't know what would have happened."

My mind was devoid of romance now, emptied like last year's bird nests. I just wanted to go home. I wasn't even sure I ever wanted to date again. If I did, though, it sure wouldn't be with Gene Matheny. I thought back to the days when I wanted to get me to the nunnery. Right now that didn't seem like such a bad idea.

Of course, I recovered, and I didn't go searching for convents. The very next week, I met Ben Fortinberry. His family had just moved to Collins and they went to church at Crossroads Missionary Baptist. He was sweet and gentle and he really did take me to see Jeremiah Johnson. *It was at the Rebel in Hattiesburg. We dated all summer and he never tried anything more than a quick kiss at the door when he took me home. Of course, Daddy did insist on answering the door holding the Mossie.*

I lie back and rub eyes that feel like they're full of ground glass. I think of Ben and those sweet summer evenings learning finally about boys and a little about a softer face of romance. Double and triple dating at the Beverly Drive-In in Hattiesburg after Daddy began to trust Ben, playing putt putt golf then eating Lot-o-Burgers at the Frost Top. There wasn't a lot to do in Collins and Daddy was all in favor of activity. And double and triple dating. My eyes close and I drift into sleep.

When I wake up, I smell coffee and I look at the clock, thinking it must be morning. It isn't. I have napped for forty minutes, and I wonder if I will ever be able to sleep through this night. Someone else is apparently having trouble as well, and, thus, the coffee downstairs. I wish not only that it was morning but that I was back in time. I wish I could walk downstairs and hear Daddy's music blaring on the radio and see Mama putting biscuits in the oven, wearing the tight look that always came around her mouth whenever the Oakridge boys sang Bed of Roses. *Mama hated country music. She liked Dean Martin and Andy Williams and had 33LPs of both of them in the console stereo Daddy had bought her for Christmas when I was twelve. Daddy, however, liked all things honkey tonk, and would put the Hanks on first thing every morning—Hank Williams and Hank Snow.*

I missed supper and I am hungry, but I can't face walking downstairs to the silence and the newness of Daddy's absence, so I reach down to the foot of the bed for the Whitman box. "Take me back, just for a little while," I whisper, and reach in the box. When I look at the small leather keeper, I smile. The little leather band was meant to hold the reins together on a mule harness, but I had worn it like a ring for a month before it went into the memory box. It was given to me by Gator Hogmueller.

GATOR HOGGMUELLER

Mama and Daddy were pretty open-minded for the times, I guess, but if Mama had still been alive, I don't think I would have been allowed to make the acquaintance of Gator Hoggmueller. As it was, my care and upbringing had been left in the hands of Daddy, Aunt Lavinia, Uncle Calvin, and Cletus—*sans* Uncle all the time now. Most of the time, I was left to my own devices, but now and then Daddy talked to me about what Mama would have wanted and reeled me in. Uncle Calvin believed I needed to be given room to be a free spirit and express myself, and Aunt Lavinia just broke into spontaneous prayer every time I came into a room. She never went against Uncle Calvin, though. Cletus just did his best to teach me about evading the government.

So when Gator Hogmueller showed up in Hot Coffee the same day we went there to spend a week with Uncle Brantley, Aunt Tiny, and all the cousins, I was able to get to know him without making much of a stir. I had gone over to the general store to get Cletus a Coke—some things never change—and there was this long, tall, skinny man coming into the parking lot in a covered wagon pulled by two black mules. I stood there with my mouth open while he got down and patted the mules. Little Abner and Daisy Mae, he called them. People sure like to be funny with names.

"Hey," I said.

"Hey, yourself."

A big Rottweiler jumped down off the wagon seat then and came over and started licking my knee. I didn't know if he wanted to be friends or try the hors d'oeuvres, but I reached down and patted him anyway. "The Duke likes you," the man said.

"Duke?"

"No, *The* Duke. And if The Duke likes you, you gotta be good people. My name's Gator Hogmueller," he said, holding out a big, rough, brown spotted hand with thick yellow fingernails. I took the hand and shook it, the callouses on the underside scratching my own soft palm.

"Pleased to meet you, Mr. Hoggmueller. My name's Evangeline Tanner, but everybody calls me Vangie. Everybody except Mama, but Mama expired last summer," I said trying to sound grown up.

"Expired? What was she, a library card?" Gator Hoggmueller bellowed, laughing and slapping his knees.

I pulled myself up to my full five feet, two inches, and started to huff off, but felt that big hand on my shoulder before I could take a second step.

"Didn't mean to offend you, little lady. Vangie. But I believe in calling a frog a frog. My mama died, too. When I was twenty-two. And my friends all call me Gator."

Being treated like an equal instead of a kid made all my mad drift away like morning fog on a hot summer day. "Why do you drive a wagon, Mr. . . . Gator? Where do you live? I've never seen you around before."

"Well, it's dang hard to hitch these mules to a car," and he was off again, slapping his knees. "Let me get a pack of Pall Malls and I'll tell you all about it."

I went in, too, and got Cletus's Coke out of the big drink box by the front window. Gator paid for it along with his cigarettes. When he pinched Mrs. Speed's cheek and called her "darlin', I was so dumbfounded I didn't even notice her opening the bottle. I was two swigs in when I remembered it was supposed to be for Cletus, but it was too late then.

"Got a place I could light for a spell, darlin'?" Gator smiled up at Mrs. Speed and added, "I'm traveling across the country and I need to rest my mules for a day or two. The scenery round here sure is purty," he added, never taking his eyes off Mrs. Speed's jowly face with the big nose.

Mrs. Speed flushed and her eyelids kind of fluttered before she said, "Well I guess you could park around back by the old garage. My husband was always a one to be kind to strangers." She handed him a box of matches and added, "My late husband, that is."

Gator thanked her for the matches and the hospitality, then went out to unhitch the mules, with me and The Duke right behind him. While he got Abner and Daisy Mae settled, I bombarded him with a steady stream of questions.

"Where do you live, Gator?"

"Right here in this wagon, little lady."

"Did you always?"

"Nope."

"Well, where did you live before?"

Gator hung the harness over the wooden fence rail, tied the mules to what he called a picket line, gave them a tub of water and a big chunk of hay, then reached in his shirt pocket for the Pall Malls. I pressed my hands down tight against my sides in fists to make myself be still and patient while he lit up. He took a deep drag on that cigarette, squinting up his eyes, then stopped breathing. I was just beginning to wonder if he was ever going to start again, when all that smoke came rolling out his nose like a bull in the Saturday cartoons. I opened my mouth to ask again just in case he had forgotten the question, but he held up one finger and sat down on the green aluminum glider in front of the barn and took another pull on the Pall Mall. I pulled up a green chair that probably matched the glider once upon a time and settled in for his tale.

Gator coughed, harked, and spit, then said, "Florida."

I waited as long as I could stand it, but he just kept smoking, staring out across the road at Mr. Fairchild's cow pasture. I looked, too, but I didn't see anything but some skinny woods cows and a rusted tractor.

"What did you do in Florida?" I finally asked.

"Wildlife management." Gator grinned. "I managed me a mess of alligators. That's how I got my name."

Okay. He was warming up now. I sipped on Cletus's coke and sat back.

"I lived in the Everglades and I knew gators. I knew how to catch 'em and I knew how to get along with 'em. Well mostly." Gator pulled up his faded denim shirt to reveal an oval made of puncture marks. Tooth prints. I shivered, and Gator said, "I think he was just playing with me."

"Why'd you leave the Everglades?" I asked, although I could think of a good number of reasons written right on Gator's side.

"Got sick." Gator took one last pull on the filterless cigarette, almost burning his fingers before he threw the butt on the ground and crushed it into the dirt with a worn brown boot. "Lung cancer," he added.

"Shouldn't you be in the hospital?" I asked. I had heard of cancer before and it wasn't something to mess around with.

"Nah," Gator said. "Nothing they can do. Doc told me to quit smoking—had some notion about cigarettes being to blame—and said I had about three months to get my affairs in order. My affairs." Gator laughed and pulled out another Pall Mall.

"But you're still smoking."

"I don't believe that hogwash. More likely it's something they're puttin' in our food. Or just nature and time, I reckon." Gator lit up with one of the matches "Darlin'" gave him. "Besides, it helps the pain. Some mornings that's the only way I can face getting up. A good cigarette and Emmy Stroud."

"Emmy Stroud?"

"Love of my life," Gator answered. "Just thinking about her makes me smile."

"Did she die?" My sense of romance was sniffing the air like a red bone hound. "And now you'll be going to join her . . ."

Gator cut me off. "Naw, she couldn't stand the sight of me. Lives in Tennessee. Married some banker feller. She sure was somethin' to look at though."

I tried to make sense of what he told me while he burned through two more cigarettes. The Duke was sitting close to Gator with his big black head resting on Gator's leg.

"Well, if you're sick, why are you all the way in Mississippi in a wagon, Gator?" I finally asked.

"I always wanted to go somewhere besides the Everglades, but never felt like I could take the time or spend the money. When I left the doctor's office I figured I still had no money and even less time, but what the he . . . the heck. I sold my little place in the Glades to one of the fellers in Wildlife, loaded my clothes in my old truck, and drove north." Gator started coughing then, and I offered him my Coke. He took a swig, wiped his mouth, and handed it back. I looked at it a minute then set the bottle on the ground beside me and leaned forward as he continued his tale.

"I got to Wakulla Springs and decided I wasn't seein' much country drivin' hell for leather—pardon my language—up the highway, so I pulled into the state park there to think a spell. I said to myself. I was always a big John Wayne fan. I said. Right out loud, mind. 'Gator, I don't think the Duke woulda done it this-a-way.'"

Right then, the Rottweiler nuzzled Gator's hand and Gator said, "Alright, boy, I'll tell her that part."

Seems Gator met the dog right in the middle of that Florida state park. The big dog just walked up to him and sat down.

"He didn't have no collar or tag," Gator said, "and I walked around lookin' for somebody that might be lookin' for him, but no luck. The feller in the park office said he'd never seen him before, so I figured the Big Chief had sent me a travelin' buddy." Gator looked heavenward to clarify then went on. "So, I named him The Duke and we piled up in the truck and went lookin' for someplace to get a burger and a milkshake. On the way, I passed a farm with a bunch of mules in the field and I come up with the idea to travel where I can go slow enough to see me some stuff and get to know some people."

Gator had traded his truck for the two mules and set off riding Lil Abner while Daisy Mae carried the duffel bags with his clothes. He made it almost to Tallahassee before he decided that riding a mule might not be the best way to travel either. He asked around and then bought a wagon from a man who was kind enough to let Gator stay in his barn while Gator rigged up some poles and a tarp to make a covered wagon.

"I'm going to Clatsop County, Oregon," Gator said and I'm going to live till I get there, then die and be done with it. Now if you'll excuse me, I better get me some supper fixins and some more Pall Malls. It was nice to meet you, little lady. You come back and see me before I go, now."

"I will. Nice to meet you, too, Gator," I said and got halfway to Aunt Tiny's before I remembered Cletus's Coke. When I got back to the store, Gator was behind his wagon setting up some kind of stove, and the mules were still munching away on the hay. I got the Coke and then walked real slow on the dirt road back to the house. I wanted to see me some stuff.

Gator never did make it to Clatsop County, Oregon. He stayed right there behind Mrs. Speed's general store for five years, smoking Pall Malls and dispensing Hogmueller wisdom. Then he died and was done with it.

I followed his example when I finally left Collins, Mississippi. I went and saw me some stuff. I still think of something he said whenever I am pondering the injustices of the world—something I do often. I had gone to see him with my young shoulders laden with unanswered questions. The World Book *held no easy answers, and Gator didn't either, really. But what he said to me has come back many times and helped me through some difficult places.*

THE TROUBLE WITH GRITS

"You goin' back to the store to see that alligator man?" Linda Sue asked. Daddy had gone back home and left me to spend two weeks with Aunt Tiny and Uncle Brantley. Linda and I were sitting at the breakfast table. Uncle Brantley and Aunt Tiny had already finished and were sitting on the front porch with their coffee. Caroline wasn't up yet and Abby, the baby of the family, was sitting at the end of the table feeding her breakfast to their dog, Cleo. I had never actually seen Abby eat and I don't know how she had lived to be ten. As the constant recipient of most of her meals, Cleo, however, looked more like a footstool than a basset hound.

I had told Linda Sue about meeting up with Gator Hogmueller over at the general store and said I figured I could learn some things about life from him. I had questions about a lot of things. The questions had been building for a long time, since I was a little girl, but it had really become a big thing to me. I'd been spending a good bit of time with Linda DeBenedetto. Daddy didn't seem to care that she was Catholic, and I just never mentioned it to Aunt Lavinia, who was a lot like Mama where religion was concerned. Jesus was a Baptist and that was that. Everybody else was headed for outer darkness and a lot of teeth gnashing. But I never forgot the things Miss Rachel had said.

Besides the whole thing about God and church and whether they were mutually exclusive, I was also doing a lot of thinking about my life and what I was going to do when I graduated. Aunt Lavinia kept asking me about boyfriends and saying how she

157

wanted to be a great aunt. Uncle Calvin, as usual, didn't say anything. Uncle Cletus said aliens were abducting women and sending back alien robot women and that was why they were getting dissatisfied with being wives and mothers. He said it was a plot to destroy the world from . . . the inside. He always paused, looked around, and lowered his voice before he said, inside.

I just told Linda I had a lot of questions about things.

"But what has that got to do with you and the alligator?"

"Gator. His name is Gator." Linda Sue always got things wrong and it aggravated me. She was a lot like Aunt Lavinia that way.

"Gator, then," she said.

"Well, I figure him dying from cancer and all, he's probably been in pretty close contact with God lately and maybe he could help me get some things straight," I said.

"I thought you didn't believe in God anymore," Linda said, pouring more Blackburn's syrup on her melted cheese biscuit.

"I believe there IS one, I just don't know that I believe Mama had it all exactly right."

I grabbed another piece of bacon and spooned tomato gravy over my opened biscuit. "I just want to see what Gator has to say. You know, learn his philosophy." Philosophy was really big with me ever since I had come across a book about it in the library. It really had my mind going in circles.

After we helped Aunt Tiny with the dishes, I slipped outside and headed down to the store. Gator was out oiling his harness when I got there.

"Hey, little lady," he called when he saw me. "Grab a rag."

I poured some Neat's Foot Oil on a piece of old tee shirt and picked up the crupper. "Gator, what do you think about God?" I asked.

He thought for a while, rubbing the oil deep into the leather of the driving reins. "I'm in favor," he said finally.

"No, I mean do you think there is one?"

"Well, how do you think all this come about if they ain't?" he replied. He inspected the rein, hung it over a tree limb, and picked up the breast collar. "It didn't just happen."

"Yeah, I think there must be a God, but if He's all powerful and all that, why did you get sick, and why did my mama die, and why do people do all the mean things they do? Why doesn't He do something about it?"

Gator put the rag down and scratched his head, but before he could answer, a cough started deep in his throat. He pulled a blue bandana out of his back pocket and coughed into it for the longest time. When he finally stopped and sat down on an overturned bucket, his face was red and sweaty and his hands were shaking.

"Well," he wheezed, "if nobody ever died, we'd be in a heck of a mess down here."

"I know, but if He's planning everything, why don't people stay well and then just die when they're really old and make way for the new ones?"

"That's some deep questions, little lady," Gator said.

"And why do people get away with being so mean to each other?" I interrupted. "And why couldn't Aunt Lavinia have children, and why is Cletus off in his head?"

"Vangie, better people than me has tried to figure all this out. Educated men. Preachers and all. All they could figure is that God is, and he made people to be people, not robots."

"Like Cletus's alien robot women," I said.

Gator stared at me like I might be off in the head, too, but he just ignored what I'd said. "If your daddy watched you all the time, every minute, and moved your arms and legs for you, and told you what to say, you might not have a lot of problems, but you wouldn't really have a life either. Maybe that's the way it is with God."

I hung the crupper from a branch and then just stood and thought about it. It kind of made sense. "Yeah," I said slowly. "I still don't know about the whole religion thing, but I can see what you mean about God. But there sure are some hard things about life."

"That's so," agreed Gator. "They's always gonna be rough patches. The trouble with life, Vangie, is the same as the trouble with grits. You ain't never gonna git all the lumps out."

Gator's simple wisdom grounds and anchors me now, just as it did back then. He was right; there are always lumps, but there is always enough good and rich and full to make it worthwhile.

I put the little leather ring on my finger. This I will keep with me, I think. The slight weight on my finger is reassuring somehow. My hand delves into the box, almost of its own accord and resurfaces with a note, the writer of which was shamelessly begging me for a date. Ah, yes, Herk Belvedere.

A STRING OF BEAUS

"Please, Vangie." Herk Belvedere had just asked me for about the umpteenth time this week to go to the movies with him.

"Herk, I've told you a hundred times I don't want to go out with you."

"You're breaking my heart, Vangie."

"And you're breaking *my* heart, Herk," said a loud voice just behind the cafeteria table where Herk had sat down beside me uninvited while I ate my lunch.

I turned and looked gratefully at Vince Hankins, the star football player for Collins High School and the man I had decided would father my children. Except that I didn't really plan to have children. But maybe Vince could change my mind, I thought dreamily as I stared into his amazingly blue eyes. Maybelline would kill for a model with lashes as thick, long, and dark as his.

I had dated Ben Fortinberry all summer after the disastrous evening with Gene Matheny, but by Labor Day we both knew we were just friends and he became a fond memory of my first for-real boyfriend. The second week of school my senior year, though, the earth turned backwards for a good two minutes when Vince sat down right in front of me in American Literature. I paid a lot more attention to his curly black hair than I ever did to Natty Bumppo. I could imagine my fingers in that hair. Only the thought of failing my last year of high school made me force myself to return to James Fennimore Cooper at all.

"Oh, hi, Vince," Herk mumbled.

I just stared up at those eyes that were staring steadily at Herk. Then I realized I had spaghetti sauce dripping down my chin. As I hastily wiped it off, Herk pushed back his chair and said he had to get to his locker, and I prayed to God and any saints that would listen to a Baptist girl that Vince would take the now unoccupied seat. He didn't. So much for saints. I sighed as he walked away, then resumed eating spaghetti, slurping a noodle up into my mouth because now it didn't matter if I sprayed sauce over my face until it looked like a giant meatball.

Mary Beth McClendon, sitting on my other side, said, "Why won't you go out with Herk? He's not awful."

"Mary Beth, I don't think 'not awful' is a good basis to start a relationship," I said, tearing my roll in half.

"I didn't say anything about a relationship." She spooned up applesauce like it was going to be outlawed any day. "Just a chance to go see a movie or play putt putt golf."

"Hmmph," I muttered and cleaned up the last of the spaghetti sauce with my roll. Mama probably did a somersault in her grave at that, as it most definitely wasn't ladylike. Aunt Lavinia didn't mind if I sopped it out of the bowl, as long as I had my pinkie extended.

"I wish Vince would ask me," I said sitting back. "I wouldn't think twice."

Mary Beth rolled her eyes, but then asked, "Well, why don't you try out for cheerleading or something?"

"For one thing, it's too late to try out. For another, I am not little or blonde or coordinated. If I managed to get up on somebody's shoulders I'd probably trip over an ear and end up killing or maiming the whole squad."

"Well at least go to the games and make sure he knows you're watching him play."

"I absolutely hate football, Mary Beth. Nothing, not even Vince, could induce me to spend hours on a hard bench watching a bunch of guys ram into each other and fall into piles on top of a football."

"Well, why do you want to go out with Vince, then? He lives and breathes football."

"Have you looked at him?"

"Well, yeah, he's cute. But that isn't enough reason to want to go out with him. What would you talk about?"

"Just because he plays football and looks like a Greek god doesn't mean he isn't smart or interesting," I retorted.

"Vangie, he has to have a tutor for wood shop."

Just then the sound of a donkey braying reverberated around the lunchroom. Mary Beth and I both turned toward the sound, incredulous. Vince, with his arm around Beverly Beehan, the smallest, blondest cheerleader in school, whispered something to Roy Atwood, then laughed, or rather brayed, again.

"If you ever do go out with him, I wouldn't tell any jokes," Mary Beth said and closed her milk carton.

I sighed again. I hated it when Mary Beth clouded the issue with facts. She was right, of course, but I still wasn't sure I wouldn't go if he asked. Just to see what a date with a Greek god was like.

He didn't ask, but Herk did. Again and again and again. One Saturday in November, when I had nothing at all to do and all my friends had dates, Herk called and said there was a great movie playing at the Cinema in Hattiesburg. What can I say? It was a weak moment and I agreed. He was coming to pick me up at five, so at four-thirty I threw on a pair of blue jeans and a sweatshirt, combed at my hair, and put on my ratty old Keds. When I answered the door, Herk said, "Ah, be sure to get your purse. It'll be Dutch."

I stared at him a moment, then said, "No, it'll be French. *Au revoir*," then slammed the door in his face.

I was still standing staring at the door in total disbelief when Daddy came out of the kitchen. "I thought you had a date," he said. Still stunned, I told him what had happened. Daddy threw back his head and laughed until he cried. After a few seconds I joined him. It was the most ridiculous thing I could imagine.

"Can you believe him?" I asked, leaning against the wall trying to catch my breath.

"French," Daddy wheezed. "Good one, Vangie."

"Yeah, well, now I'm stuck at home on a Saturday night," I said, wiping my eyes.

Daddy reached in his pocket and threw me the keys to the Bel Air. "Take yourself to the movies, Vangie. Or go down to Sandy's and get a bite to eat."

I thought about it for a minute, then said, "Why not? I can go out without a date."

As I opened the door, Daddy said, "You gonna change clothes, Vangie?"

"Nope," I answered stepping outside. "I hope the outfit will discourage Dutch suitors."

I heard Daddy laughing again as I walked to the driveway. I felt well on my way to being a liberated single woman.

Liberation and ideas of being single lasted about as long as it took me to get a table at Sandy's Fish House in Mount Olive. I was doodling on my napkin when the waiter came over, a nice looking boy with brown hair and browner eyes. I looked up at him and smiled.

"You an artist?" he asked.

"Aren't you supposed to ask me what I want to drink?" I said haughtily. "Ice tea with lemon, and be quick about it."

He flushed. "Yes, ma'am," he said and turned to go.

"Wait," I said, "I'm sorry. I was going for witty banter, but I guess it just came off rude. I'm not terribly good at the whole flirty thing."

"Well, no, if that was flirting, you're not," he agreed. "So, *are* you an artist?"

I looked at the napkin, which had a reasonable facsimile of the large, florid hostess on it. "I like to draw, but I don't know that I could be called an artist."

"My professor says loving it is the first and most important thing," he said.

"Your professor?"

"Yeah. I'm a freshman at Southern Miss in Hattiesburg. Majoring in fine art. I better go get your drink. I'll be quick about it," he added, but he smiled. "I'm Jamie," he called over his shoulder.

Jamie came back with the tea, a bowl of coleslaw, and a dish of hushpuppies. "I'm Vangie, short for Evangeline," I said as he set the dishes down.

"What can I get you, Vangie, short for Evangeline?"

"The seafood platter. Fried." I was dressed like a refugee and had insulted him within seconds of meeting him. I saw no need to try to impress him with my dainty manners and ladylike appetite at this point.

When he brought out the steaming platter piled high with catfish, shrimp, oysters, and a stuffed crab, he said, "I was just getting off work. You're my last customer. Mind if I sit with you?"

"Not at all." I thumped the catsup bottle trying to dislodge its contents. This worked rather well, sending a healthy spray of red onto my sweatshirt.

I was just beginning to wonder if it was scientifically possible for a person to actually die of mortification when Jamie grabbed a shrimp off my plate, daubed it in the catsup blob on my shirt, and said, "Now that's handy."

Laughing, I wiped the catsup off my shirt and dug into the food. I had polished off the shrimp and was halfway through with the stuffed crab when I realized I wasn't the least bit self-conscious with Jamie. I had actually forgotten what a straggly mess I was and Jamie didn't even seem to notice it.

He told me he was Jamie Derrickson from Florence, Miss., but his family had moved to Mount Olive in his junior year of high school.

"I'm getting some of my core courses done, and I'm taking one art class, Drawing 1," he said. "But I really want to go to Europe to study."

"I plan to go to college," I said, "but first, I want to travel." I thought of Gator Hogmueller, and added, "I want to see some stuff."

"What do you plan to study when you do go?" Jamie asked.

"I'm not sure," I said." I'm interested in so many things it's hard to decide on just one."

"I know exactly what I want to do," Jamie said, and his face just lit up. "I want to paint. Like Rembrandt or Vermeer. They're Dutch . . .what's wrong!"

Jamie had jumped up, his eyes as big as the coleslaw bowl, as I coughed and choked. "Dutch," I managed, laughing so hard the oyster that had been almost lodged in my throat popped out onto the table.

"What's wrong with Dutch?" he asked like I'd told him his mother was an orangutan.

I tried to compose myself, but then he added, "Derrickson is a Dutch name."

I slapped the table, almost hysterical now. "You, you're, you're . . . Dutch," I managed, sliding down in my chair, but with enough presence of mind to pray that he would stay long enough for me to explain.

The Trouble with Grits

"Evangeline!" my aunt Helen calls, reaching new decibel levels. She is probably calling me that way because I have slept through her less shrill attempts. It is morning and I am surprised that I have slept through the night. I am equally surprised to see I am still holding the napkin drawing from the fish house; I had dug it out of the box, remembering that evening. I scoot slowly to the side of the bed, and maybe because my bones feel like they are made of overcooked noodles, I recall the time when I was ten or so and Mama came into my room to wake me.

I had opened my eyes on that occasion and without a word slid from the bed onto the floor and, flat on my belly, arms plastered to my sides, began to work my way across the room like a giant worm. "What?" was all she could get out. "I'm feeling sluggish," I had replied, and continued across the floor. Mama had stared at me like she believed I had, indeed, morphed into some unsavory variety of garden creature. If Daddy had been the one to wake me, I am sure he would have created some game of trying to "exterminate me," or at the very least would have had something funny to say. Mama was apparently born without a sense of humor, or had since had it surgically removed. Feeling foolish instead of witty, I had gotten up from the floor, walked past her where she was still standing transfixed, and, with as much dignity as I could muster, made my way down the hall.

Today, I feel no inclination to be witty. "Evangeline," Aunt Helen calls again. "Breakfast." I go to the door, and seeing her standing at the bottom of the stairs, say, "I'll be down in a minute, Aunt Helen."

When I get downstairs, intending to have only a cup of the coffee that had beckoned me the minute I opened my bedroom door, I see immediately that this is not a viable plan. Aunt Lavinia has made

Company Breakfast. I'm pretty sure snubbing that labor of love is the unpardonable sin.

One glimpse of a company breakfast in Covington County, Mississippi would cause Shoney's breakfast bars across the nation to shut down in abject mortification. Aunt Lavinia has the long dining table laden fit for the Second Coming. Bowls and platters of eggs—scrambled, over easy, and sunny side up—are nestled among platters of bacon and country ham. Steam fried potatoes sit beside a huge plate of fried chicken and a bowl of milky chicken gravy. Another bowl, this one filled with tomato gravy, is near a platter of hot biscuits. Just in case some finicky palate is reluctant to partake of any of these offerings, stacks of pancakes and buttered toast are laid out near syrup, honey, and molasses, along with preserves, jams, and jellies wrought from every fruit imaginable, including scuppernongs and mayhaws. A pound cake with sugared strawberries and whipped cream are on the buffet for anyone who wants to eat light! And, of course, in the middle of the table, holding court as it were, is a huge steaming pot of buttered grits.

I help my plate as though I am actually hungry, then spoon grits into a small bowl. One tiny lump is barely visible in the very center of the dish. I smile, remembering Gator, and take a long fond look at my perfectly imperfect family. Then I think of Jamie and all the lumps in that relationship as it grew. Then again, I may have been the only lump, and I was often more like a speedbump, or a concrete highway barrier. I specifically remember another breakfast at this same large dining table years ago. The bounty, then, was not as plentiful as now, but the meal and the events leading up to it were just as life changing as the happenings of these past few days.

SPEED BUMPS AND SEEIN' STUFF

"I want to go with you," I insisted.

"Vangie, we've talked about this. You need to go to college, decide what you want to do. I'll be gone for a year, then I'll be back. And I'll come home for the holidays. It won't be so bad."

Jamie and I had been together since the night at the fish house, and I hated the thought of being away from him for a whole year. Besides, I had no intention of starting college yet. I was determined to travel, see stuff, like Gator had said.

"I'm going to Europe," I said. "I've got enough saved to pay my way."

"I'm going to be studying, Vangie. And we aren't ready to get married yet anyway."

"I never said a thing about getting married." I had said yes when Jamie proposed right after graduation, but I never said when. "I *am* going. With you or by myself."

Jamie sighed deeply. "I can't take care of you, Vangie. This is a study abroad program and I'll be living in a dorm and I won't even be working."

"I know all that, Jamie. I am going to travel because I want to. And I'm going to see England first because that is where you'll be. But I have a plan and I'll take care of myself."

"How?" he asked.

Not having a really good answer, I chose silence. It's not that I didn't have a plan. Of sorts. I was just that it was only half formed and I knew perfectly well he wouldn't approve.

Jamie sighed, then took a long deep breath. He seemed to do that a lot. I wondered absently if he had an oxygen deficiency. "Listen," he said, "even if I agreed that you should go . . . now wait," he added hastily as he saw what Daddy called my dander beginning to rise. "I don't mean agree like permission, I just mean even if I thought this was a good idea, it takes time to get a passport and you have to get a ticket and I'll be leaving in less than a week. It just won't work out, Vangie. I'm sorry."

I had made up my mind, even though it seemed like everybody in the family was determined to talk me out of it. Well, everybody that I had told, which was only my cousins. Except my cousin Denver Reardon. He's always encouraged me to be true to myself and go after what I want out of life. Aunt Lavinia, on the other hand, thought my engagement to Jamie meant that God had finally answered her unceasing prayers and divine intervention had brought me to my senses. She had mentioned several times what beautiful children Jamie and I would have. Childless, she depended on me to produce great-nieces and -nephews to serve as grandchildren for her.

"Sorry to disappoint you, old girl," I said now, to Jamie's obvious bewilderment. He, however, had grown used to bewilderment since dating me and said nothing.

"I'm going. That's that," I said and got up off the front porch step. "See you tonight?"

I know I heard "pig headed," but I wasn't sure if it was followed by mule or fool. When I turned around, Jamie smiled up at me, so I chose to think I imagined it.

After I got out Daddy's old suitcase, I began making a list of things I should take. I looked in my nightstand drawer and touched the blue passport book. I had gotten it months ago when Jamie started talking seriously about studying abroad. I had every intention of needing a passport, though, whether Jamie ever stepped foot outside Covington County or not. Just looking at it made my stomach lurch in anxious, but happy anticipation. I was doing this.

I had seen all Jamie's travel documents and had managed to get a ticket on the same flight. Jamie was going to stay with his aunt and uncle in Florence, Mississippi the week before he was to leave, so he wouldn't have any idea what was happening until I showed up at the airport, and then it would be too late. I planned to tell Daddy and everybody that I was going, but not until Jamie was safely tucked away in Florence.

My plan was to backpack through Europe. That was as far as I had gotten, not being able to find much information on exactly how to go about it. I wanted to see Ireland and Scotland and walk on the lands where the Sullivans and MacRaes had lived. Maybe meet some distant relatives. Then I was going to Germany, and Austria where that new movie with Julie Andrews was set. Oh I just knew those hills would be alive. And Switzerland. I had seen *Heidi* and couldn't wait to explore little mountain villages. Of course, I wanted to see France and Italy and go to the Louvre and see the Sistine chapel. If I was destined to be an artist, I figured it would be revealed to me there. And of course, I needed to see Paris where all kinds of writers lived. And then there was Verona, Romeo and Juliet's hometown. I'd heard about bullfights in Spain, and wanted to check that out. Not that I wanted to be a bullfighter. Heck I didn't even like the bull riding in the rodeo in Jackson at the Dixie National. But I still wanted to see Spain. Then I'd go back to London to be with Jamie until he was done with school.

I had bought a big backpack and some good walking shoes and I had a map I cut out of the Atlas. I was the only one who looked at the Atlas, so I figured it wouldn't be missed. The only thing I found after searching the library, magazine stand, and book section of the drug store was that there were these places called hostels and you could stay there really cheap. The hippies were going to India and places like that, but that's not what I wanted. I had some money left after the ticket and shoes and backpack, but I knew I'd have to work along the way. Doing what I wasn't sure, but something was bound to turn up.

I knew Daddy and Jamie would both throw a hissy fit if I told them what I had in mind. I wouldn't lie, but I could manipulate the truth a little. I would tell them about the hostel in London; I just wouldn't mention that I was only staying there for two weeks, then heading out to see some stuff. I had the names of a few more hostels in countries all over Europe. When I took time to think about it, I was a tiny bit afraid of being on my own, so I just didn't think about that part. I thought, instead, about all the places and things I would see. And I planned to make the big life decisions while I was there.

Jamie was over every night for the next week, acting all droopy about leaving me, and I tried to act sad, too, but I was so excited I had a hard time pretending to be heartbroken. I noticed him looking at me confused and a little hurt a couple of times, so I tried harder. I drove him to his aunt's house in Florence on the next to the last Friday in August. We went on up to Jackson and he took me to dinner at this really nice restaurant there. He kept looking at me, all hound dog eyes, and holding on to my hand. I tried to work up some tears, but the effect was ruined when I giggled a little thinking about how it would be when I showed up at the Jackson International Airport with my suitcase and passport in hand. He dropped my hand and started picking at his steak. I felt bad for him, but I didn't dare say anything, so I just ate my prime rib and ordered the coconut cream pie for dessert.

After dinner, I dropped him at his Aunt Gwen's house and kissed him goodbye. I didn't have to fake tears then, because I was sad that we would be apart for even a week. He seemed to feel a lot better when I cried, and he hugged me hard to him and told me he loved me and would miss me something awful. I smiled into his shoulder, and hugged him back, then left to get back home before Aunt Lavinia called the sheriff's office to check accident reports. She was a worrier.

When I got up the next morning, I decided it was time to spill. I figured I best lead up to it gently. If I just blurted out that I planned to tramp around Europe like a Gypsy, Aunt Lavinia might go into terminal vapors. Or Daddy might lock me in the attic until I was twenty-one. So I planned my strategy, then came downstairs in white gloves and one of Aunt Lavinia's hats. Trying to sound like Haley Mills, I said, "Lovely morning, what?" Nothing. It was like Haley came to breakfast every day. I tried again. "Have you any marmalade? Everyone in London just adores marmalade."

"Yeah, well, folks in Collins like dewberry jelly," said Daddy, putting a biscuit on my plate.

"It'll stain those gloves, Vangie. Better take 'em off," put in Aunt Lavinia.

I took off the gloves and buttered the biscuit morosely. This wasn't going exactly like I planned. Maybe I better be a little more direct. "A year in London would certainly ground a person," I tried. "A person would have some experiences, be able to make better decisions."

"I think it'll be good for Jamie," said Daddy.

"And it will give you time to work on your hope chest," said Aunt Lavinia. "You haven't embroidered a single pillow case as far as I know."

Then Daddy started talking to Uncle Calvin about putting in some blueberry bushes and I gave up. Until dinner.

"I'll make dessert," I offered a few hours later as Aunt Lavinia was putting cornbread in the oven. We always had a big dinner straight up noon on Saturdays and then most everybody ate cornbread and milk for supper.

"That's a sweet girl," cooed Aunt Lavinia. She loved it whenever I showed any signs of domesticity.

I had copied a recipe for crepes and I sang *Frere Jacques* as I mixed the batter. After we ate roast, gravy, mashed potatoes, and pink-eyed purple hull peas with cornbread crumbled in the pot liquor, I got up to finish the crepes.

"*Les crepes*," I announced in my best Brigitte Bardot impersonation.

"Pancakes?" asked Uncle Cletus, eyeing my masterpiece with nothing short of disdain. "For dessert? Git me some ice cream, girlie."

"*Mais non*," I said using the only French words I could recall besides *bon jour* and *au revoir*. "Ze crepes are . . ." I searched. "*Magnifique*! You will adore zem."

"Vangie," Daddy interjected patiently, while eyeing the beret and velvet choker I had donned in the kitchen. "Let's stick to American. I'll try some of them pancakes."

After I had served everyone a plate of crepes, along with the ice cream Uncle Cletus insisted on, I went upstairs and brought down my sketch book and pencils.

"I'd like to capture this moment on canvas," I said as I began to draw.

"This?" Uncle Cletus said, not bothering to swallow before he spoke.

"This moment of family breaking bread together," I said. "Before the daughter of the house goes off to start her own life." I continued to draw.

"Well, there'll be a bunch more bread breaking before the wedding," Aunt Lavinia put in. "These pancakes are pretty good. How'd you get 'em so thin?"

I ignored her. "You know," I said, striving for afterthought, "Some of the most famous artists were French. I sure could learn a lot by visiting the Louvre."

"The loo?" Daddy stopped with the fork halfway to his mouth.

"The Louvre," Uncle Calvin said, enunciating. "In Paris. It's the most important museum in France." He eyed me thoughtfully.

Thinking I might be tipping my hand prematurely, I remained silent, turning my attention to Aunt Lavinia as she stuck her head forward and swallowed visibly and audibly.

"Hey there's a museum of some sort in Jackson," Daddy said. "It might not be the Loo, but it's closer."

Only slightly discouraged, I packed up my pencils and went back upstairs to plan my next move. At least maybe I had planted a seed. I'd leave it overnight to germinate. Denver was in town, so I called him to fill him in on progress.

The next morning, I came down to breakfast determined this was the day to get it out and over with. As it happened, Aunt Helen had shown up at supper time with Aunt Tiny and Uncle Brantley. Coincidence? Maybe, but really I figured it was ordained, that God, in His mercy, was making sure I would only have to go through this one time.

I waltzed in singing in full voice, "The Hills are Alive," just as the grits went on the table.

"Quit that caterwauling, girl," exclaimed Uncle Brantley, who had been sitting closest to the door when I came in, and had jumped and dropped the egg he was trying to slide onto his plate. The yolk broke and was oozing bright yellow over the white plastic table cloth.

My face flushed as I went silent, but soon I was humming *Edelweiss*, as I repositioned the white scarf I had tied over my head. Everyone resumed eating. Subtlety was lost on this family. So I broke into *The Lonely Goatherd*, yodeling spectacularly.

Seven startled faces turned to me and on impulse I stood up and announced loudly, "I'm going to Europe. With Jamie."

Aunt Lavinia had just put a big bite of ham in her mouth and started coughing violently, which diverted the attention from me for the moment. I hurried to get her some water as I figured a big gulp of the scalding hot coffee by her plate would do her in, and Uncle Calvin jumped up to do the Heimlich maneuver, should it be necessary. Aunt Helen, unperturbed, said brightly, "The hog always get choked." This made Aunt Lavinia slap out at her and the motion seemed to dislodge the ham. With Aunt Lavinia safely removed from death's door, all eyes turned back to me. I was dipping a piece of crunchy fried hoecake into a pool of peanut butter syrup, feigning nonchalance and pretending I didn't notice the silence or the staring. Neither nonchalance nor silence was destined to last for long, though.

"You're what?" Daddy said standing up and leaning over the table with his hands gripping the edge.

At the same time, Uncle Cletus started muttering something about spies, and Aunt Lavinia was crying out, "Heaven's a Day," while Uncle Calvin was beginning a diatribe about the importance of an education. Aunt Tiny was asking about the wedding, not even considering that I would be such a bold, brazen hussy as to travel with a man without benefit of marriage, and Uncle Brantley asked Daddy if he was going to let me run off with that boy. Over the cacophony, which sounded like the proverbial long tailed cats in a room full of rocking chairs, Aunt Helen was asking loudly if I was going to see Buckingham Palace.

I looked from one to the other, not knowing who to answer first, then figured it had best be Daddy. "I've made up my mind, Daddy, and I've got everything worked out. I'm going to London with Jamie and stay in a hostel, that's a really cheap hotel, and do some sightseeing and I'll come back with him when his program is over in June."

Daddy was silent, but he was the only one. Everyone else continued talking all at the same time, each getting louder trying to be heard over each other.

". . . because there is so little time to get the invitations out or buy a dress. . ."

". . . university there, I suppose, but it's almost. . ."

". . .a disguise. Maybe that's the way . . ."

". . .in her grave, I tell you. I'm about to faint myself. . ."

". . . disgrace. At least Otis eloped and didn't just go off. . ."

". . . and there's Big Ben. Oh I'd love to see it all, except I can't see a damn thing. . ."

I was feeling a little queasy, and Daddy took my arm and led me out of the kitchen and into the back yard.

"What's the meaning of this, Vangie?" he said, his mouth tight and his eyes narrowed. Daddy had never looked or sounded like this to me before and I felt my stomach knot up and thought I might lose the hoecake. Before I could answer, the back door swung open and Denver strode out, with all the previous occupants of the breakfast table fluttering out behind him like so many hens following the rooster.

He always did have good timing, I thought, grateful for the interruption. Gratitude turned to adoration and awe at his next words. "I've come to help Vangie get ready for our trip."

"Our. . ." I said then stopped as he glared toward me briefly before continuing. "I assume she told you that she wants to go to England with Jamie, and of course, she can't go off unescorted. Everyone nodded, kind of numbly, I thought, but I caught right on. Dear, darling Denver. He apparently foresaw the turmoil that would ensue when I unveiled my plans, which I had shared with him only a day or two before, and had again come riding in to save the day.

"Oh well, yes," Daddy said. "She just now nearly killed us all at breakfast springing it on us from out of nowhere. But she didn't say a thing about you going, too, Denver."

"Judging from the way it sounded when I came in, nobody would have heard her if she did. Now let's get back inside. I'm starving and it looks like I'm just in time."

Oh, how right he was.

Breakfast that day is just as clear in my memory as this one. I look around at these people I love so dearly and have a little pang at the grief and worry I caused them—and not just that day. Aside from Denver, only Aunt Helen really applauded me and my adventures. I wrote to her regularly while I was in Europe and she responded with enthusiasm and encouragement. Occasionally, Linda Sue, who was commissioned to read and write for her since Uncle Jules had passed away, would throw in her own negative comments, which I interpreted as petty jealousy.

After I've eaten, I get another cup of coffee just to stay with these, the people closest to me. None of us have much to say this morning, and that suits my mood. I'm still lost in the mists of the past, from all the hours spent in the memory box I suppose, but I am not ready to come back to now. Not just yet. I try to help Aunt Lavinia with the mountain of dishes that resulted from the cooking and eating of Company Breakfast. She, of course, refuses, saying Helen can help her and sends me out of the room, offering me cold compresses and sweet tea, like my maladies are of the body not the soul. I go back upstairs, intending to take a bath and dress and get ready to move out of the past and back into my life as it is now. Instead, I dip my hand back into the Whitman box, searching for solace in memory. As luck would have it, I pick up my ticket to England.

ENGLAND SWINGS
LIKE A PENDULUM DO

"There he is," I shouted at Denver. "At the Delta ticket counter."

He winced. "Vangie, I'm right beside you. Have you been taking elocution lessons from Helen?"

I lowered my voice, but Jamie apparently heard me over the din of the busy airport, and turned incredulously and looked from me to Denver and back to me again like we were two French jugglers caught sneaking in to a Presidential Inaugural Ball.

"Sir," I heard the counter attendant say as I dragged Denver over to join the line behind Jamie. "I need your identification, please. You're holding up the other passengers."

Jamie forced his attention back, completed checking his luggage in, and then walked back to where Denver and I were moving up in the queue.

"Vangie, what on Earth?" he spluttered.

"I told you I was coming, too," I said. I could feel the grin all the way across my face like an upturned slice mark into a Thanksgiving ham.

"But, what? How?"

"Apparently, she's been planning this for months, pal," Denver answered for me. I couldn't get my lips close enough together for intelligible speech. I did manage to nod enthusiastically though.

"I don't believe it," Jamie said. "And you, Denver? You're coming too?"

Denver scratched his head, then took a toothpick out of his shirt pocket before answering. "Well, I could imagine the uproar when Vangie told her Daddy and the rest of the herd that she planned to take off alone and backp. . . Ow!"

I pinched Denver to shut him up. It was enough to get Jamie past the idea that I was boarding that plane with him. I didn't know what he would do when he heard the rest of my plan, but I didn't want to find out right then.

Comprehending, Denver amended, "So I decided to come along too and help her find her way and get settled. You know there's no stopping her when she's got her mind made up, don't you, boy?" Denver put the toothpick in his mouth.

Resigned, Jamie said, "Don't I know it, man." But then his face lit up as he shifted mental gears and found traction on the fact that we wouldn't be parted for the next year after all.

"Could you move ahead, buddy?" said a short, round man with what looked like gravy on his light blue tie. We all shoved suitcases and moved forward in line. When we stopped, Jamie grabbed me and hugged me hard. "You're a little insane, you know that?" he said, but his smile nearly matched my own now.

"You've seen my family," I answered. "What did you expect?"

We finally got on the 727 that would take us to The John F. Kennedy International Airport in New York City, and even though our assigned seats were far apart from each other, there were enough empty ones that we found a row where we could all sit together. I had never been on an airplane before and was fascinated with everything and I'm sure I talked a mile a minute. Jamie was just as enthused, but this was all old hat to Denver and he was content to be our travel mentor.

A stewardess came by with a cart and I had my first taste of champagne. It was bubbly and sweeter than the Shabbat wine that

Miss Rachel used to let me sip, and can you believe it was free? Denver had a second glass, but I felt a little light headed after the first and was afraid I might be allergic. When the stewardess was refilling Denver's glass, I asked if I could meet the pilot. Jamie elbowed me, but the stewardess said, "Sure!' and took me right to the cockpit and introduced me to a man she called the captain. He let me sit in one of the chairs up there. It was covered in some soft, fleecy material and was really comfortable. I stayed about five minutes asking questions about all the instruments and then had to go back to my seat.

"You wouldn't believe what it was like in there," I exclaimed when I returned. "Switches and lights and knobs all across the cockpit. I don't know how he remembers which ones do what."

Jamie apparently wasn't allergic to the champagne and was sipping on a fresh glass and nodding and smiling at me as I went on about it all.

Denver leaned back and closed his eyes and Jamie took out some papers and started going through them. I had taken the aisle seat so I could look around without bothering the boys, and I kept finding reasons I needed to get up and walk around and I think the stewardess knew I was new to all this and she showed me the galley, and pointed out the tiny little powder rooms. I wondered momentarily if there was a septic tank on the bottom of the plane. I stopped and sat by a woman with two little kids. She looked really tired and the kids were popping around like jack-in-the-boxes, so I played games with them for a little while till they got tired and were ready to sit still.

Then I went back to my seat, but I kept swiveling my head around like the lazy susan on Aunt Tiny's dining room table so I could look at all the people. I was imagining where they came from and where they might be going.

It seemed like no time before we were landing in New York City. "What is that?" I cried as we barreled down the runway toward something that looked kind of like a flying saucer.

"It's the Worldport," answered Denver. "The Pan Am terminal." We disembarked and inside the terminal was all glass and metal with tall, tall ceilings held up with huge metal columns, and it was full of people going places, having adventures. If this was just the airport, I sure did wish we had time to go explore the city, but. . . another time. There was a big sign announcing that Pan Am was the "World's Most Experienced Airline." I thought that was really good to know.

We had a late dinner, they called it lunch, at a dining room there in the terminal that overlooked the whole concourse. I was so excited and interested in watching the people that I could hardly eat. In a couple of hours, we were boarding another jet, this time a 747 that would take us from New York straight to Heathrow airport in London. Again, we found three empty seats and were able to stay together. Not too long after we took off, a stewardess came through with a cart that had a big old beef roast on it and she carved it right there in the aisle. It was like a fancy restaurant right in the middle of an airplane. We had cloth napkins and everything. They had this horseradish sauce that was really good, but it made my nose burn and my eyes water. Denver said nobody was allergic to champagne, so I had another glass after dinner and got a little lightheaded again. I quit chattering and was thinking about what London would be like and the first thing I knew, my head dropped and I jerked back up. Despite my excitement, apparently the adventures of the day, and maybe the champagne, had caught up with me and I had fallen asleep, even though it was only about nine o'clock at night. When another stewardess came by and gave us blankets and pillows, Jamie and Denver told me to stretch out across the seats and sleep. They would take a couple of empty seats a few rows away.

I woke up to the sound of the captain announcing that the temperature in London was 64 degrees and reminding passengers to set their watches to the correct time, 6:12 a.m. My watch said it was just past midnight, and I was still sleepy, but I went to the powder room and splashed water on my face to try to wake up. I got back to my seat just before the final descent to Heathrow. Jamie and Denver were back on our row, and I could see out the window as we landed.

"Stay close to me," Denver told Jamie and me as we got ready to get off the plane. We got our luggage and made our way to Customs. "Top o' the morning,' guvna," I said to a man in the line ahead of us. "Stop that," Denver whispered gruffly, and I wondered who had kicked *his* cat. Maybe he was sleep deprived, too.

We made it through Customs with no problems and dragged our suitcases out onto the street. Denver hailed a cab, a funny looking vehicle with a driver dressed in a formal uniform and sitting on the wrong side of the car. Denver told the driver to take us to the Hotel Russell where we all had rooms for the night before we went our separate ways. Denver said a nice room was his gift to me before I started experiencing life in a hostel. His smile was almost nasty when he said it, but there was no way anyone could dampen my spirits.

I couldn't believe all the cars, trucks, and cabs tooling around the London streets. Of course, my frame of reference was Collins, Mississippi, where two pickups and a Buick constituted a traffic jam. I saw double-decker buses, just like I had read about, and a whole lot of people walking too. Watching it all, I just thought I'd bust a gut, as Aunt Helen says. Thinking of her, I impulsively cried out, "Can we go by Big Ben, please?"

"Bit out o' the way, luv," the driver answered, then looked at Denver, who had taken a seat up front.

"We're in no hurry. Let's go see Big Ben."

About an hour later, I was outside staring mesmerized up at the huge, ornate clock tower. "I want to hear it chime, Denver. What time is it?"

It was eight minutes before the hour, but I convinced both Denver and the cab driver to wait until I could hear the nine booming chimes that resonated all the way down to my toes. I took the new Kodak Instamatic camera out of my bag and snapped pictures from every angle. I moved back and forth until I had a shot would that would show most of the detail of the ornate clock tower. "This is for you, Aunt Helen," I said softly.

I root around in the box, purposely hunting now, all thoughts of serendipity and happenstance forgotten, and find the faded picture of Big Ben. I had described every detail to Aunt Helen, who was as proud as if she'd been there herself. I stand up and dump everything on the bed, sifting through the pictures, ribbons, bits of paper, and God knows what all to find everything I can of that pivotal year in Europe, that year when everything coalesced.

I pick up a picture of that first hostel and remember my surprise when I discovered no linens were provided. I had slept on my cotton robe and used my all-weather coat as a blanket. Knit shirts served as bath cloths and towels. I spent the second day re-evaluating and revamping the contents of my pack, wisely asking Denver's advice. He kindly offered to take back to the states with him my large suitcase and much of what I had brought.

That first week was idyllic, with Denver showing me around London while Jamie was in class and the three of us going out together each evening until exhaustion forced Jamie back to the dorm, me to my hostel, and Denver to his nice hotel room that actually had sheets, towels, and soap. (We were there for the King Tutankhamen Exhibit and for a brief time I envisioned myself wearing safari clothes and brushing dirt off some priceless artifact.) But when Denver said he was leaving, Jamie and I had our first real fight. Jamie tried to make me go back to Mississippi with Denver. When I refused and laid out my whole plan to him, you would have thought I said I was going to dance naked through the streets and sacrifice small children at midnight. In the end he huffed back to the university and I cried myself to sleep. In his pocket was the engagement ring I had flung at him when he said no wife of his was going to go tramping around Europe alone like some brazen nomad hippie kook.

The next morning he was back, skipping his first class to come find me at the little café where I had tea and scones every morning. He apologized and ask me to take back the ring. He didn't understand my decision, he said, but he would support me no matter how crazy I might be. This was to become a recurring theme.

I had decided to go on to Scotland instead of exploring England on my own. Jamie had agreed to take an extra week after the school year ended so we could sightsee together then. This was our last day together for a while and it was dimmed around the edges a little by the knowledge that I would be leaving and also because I knew Jamie disapproved and worried about me, though he was determined to be supportive. The next morning, Jamie came to the hostel and helped me carry my heavy pack downstairs. We had tea, scones, clotted cream, and tears for breakfast, then it was time to go. After hugging me long and hard, he picked up my pack, positioned it on my back, and we began the short walk to the rail station where I would begin this journey.

PEACE, BABY

"Jamie, can we go by Scotland yard?" I asked.

"Well, it's not really on the way."

We had left my hostel on Old Pye Street (I love that name. It's fun just to say it. Old Pye). Anyway, we were walking to Piccadilly Circus Station, where I planned to catch a train to Glasgow, Scotland.

"Come on, Jamie. It's not that far. Imagine being Sherlock Holmes and working with Scotland Yard solving murders and jewelry heists and stuff. Wouldn't that be amazing?"

He looked at me quizzically. "Vangie, you do know Sherlock Holmes is just fiction, right?"

"Of course," I answered disdainfully, but the truth was that for a moment there I was worked up enough to forget Sherlock wasn't a living, breathing detective.

We turned onto Tothill Street and I squeezed Jamie's hand, realizing he had taken us off the route to Piccadilly. In a few minutes, I was gazing up at the New Scotland Yard sign and wondering about old Scotland Yard at number 4 Whitehall and imagining Sherlock and Watson calling me in to confer on a case.

Jamie interrupted this pleasant reverie. "We gotta go, Vangie. You don't want to miss your train."

"Just one more thing, Jamie. Can we go to Baker Street? I want to see what's at 221B. I know," I said when I saw Jamie's expression, "Sherlock Holmes was never really there. But I still want to go see it."

When we finally got to the Piccadilly Circus station, I discovered it was a subway not a regular train station. That's what I get for not asking questions. "How could you not know?" Jamie asked. "Where did you get your ticket?"

"I don't have a ticket," I replied. "I figured I would just get one when we got here." Jamie was silent as we found a bus route from Piccadilly to Euston Road, where, we were informed, we would find the West Coast Main Line. There, I could catch the train to Charing Cross, Glasgow. We had to change buses once along the way and when we got to the Euston Station, we could see the train headed off toward Scotland. Before Jamie could start a new lecture on the virtues of planning, I ascertained that another train would leave in a little over an hour.

Jamie didn't say much, but I figured he was thinking that without guidance I'd probably end up lost in the Scottish countryside, wandering aimlessly for the rest of creation. I determined that I would become a wiser traveler and show him just what a capable, independent woman I was.

As we waited for the train, a group of people about my age, and all carrying backpacks, came into the station and got tickets for the same train. "I'm going to go talk to them," I said.

I quickly struck up a conversation and learned they had already been backpacking around most of the places I planned to go and Scotland and Ireland were the last places they planned to visit before heading back to the states and some commune in Washington. "See, Jamie?" I said, when I returned to sit by him on the bench. "Everything will be fine. Rainbow and Starlight will teach me what I need to know. Don't worry."

Apparently traveling with hippies was only a little better in Jamie's estimation than wandering the hillsides with the sheep for eternity, but he reluctantly left me in their care as we boarded the 13:40 for Charing Cross.

I got settled in on the train and Rainbow started rifling through her pack. "Oh no!" she cried. "I left the toothbrush in Newhaven."

"Good job, Rainbow," said Cosmic River, a tall good looking boy about nineteen or twenty. "Hey, Vangie, you got a tooth brush?"

"Yeah," I answered.

"Problem solved," River said to the group. "Vangie has one."

"Wait," I said. "How does that solve your problem?"

"We have to travel light. So we share everything. Rainbow has—or had—the toothbrush. Starlight has a bar of soap. Autumn has a hair bush. Like that."

"Oh," was all I said, but I made a mental note to buy an extra toothbrush I could keep hidden in my pack. I didn't want to insult my new friends and end up with the sheep, but I would let my teeth fall out before I would share a tooth brush.

I learned a lot from my own personal rainbow coalition. I tried taking a hit of marijuana, but instead of getting high I got sick and threw up on Gentle Dream's sandals. They never offered me any more MJ, as they called it, but they did teach me about hitchhiking and camping, as well as navigating one's way out of a herd of sheep in the middle of the road in Limerick, Ireland.

I look through a few pictures of those days with my hippies. We had visited ancient castles and explored standing stones in Scotland, then took the ferry from Troon, Scotland to Larne in Northern Ireland. We hitchhiked mostly, taking cars, trucks, and at one point an oxcart, from place to place. We kissed the Blarney Stone, explored more ancient castles and traveled the Ring of Kerry. I met plenty of Sullivans in County Cork and raised a pint at a number of pubs. My pints contained hard cider; stout made me gag.

I had learned to share linens, soap, shampoo, and a tent. But I drew a hard line at the toothbrush. I had taken to keeping it in my bra after I found Peaceful Day loading it up with my toothpaste. I had snagged it just before she got it to her mouth.

As I put the pictures to the side, I see a postcard, the only thing I had kept from Munich.

THE GIRL FROM U.N.C.L.E.

"Get a rail pass," whispered Summer Night, as I hugged her goodbye in Dublin. The hippies were flying back to the States and I was catching a ferry to Manchester where I would make my way back to London to spend a day or two with Jamie.

"A rail pass?" I asked. "And why are you whispering?"

"River thinks hitching is the only pure way to travel, unless you have no other choice," she whispered. "But you shouldn't be hitching on your own. You can get a rail pass pretty cheap in London, and you can use it to get pretty much anywhere you want."

River had by silent coup or something become the leader of the group and the rest of us just followed blindly, or at least I did. I didn't know there were viable alternatives to hiking and traveling with sheep, but now I was a little annoyed with myself that I hadn't at least asked.

"Thanks, Summer," I said, hugging her once more.

"Be sure you get to Munich for Oktoberfest," she called as she rejoined the group and I turned away to get on the ferry. "It's already started, so you need to get there pretty quick."

Without River's dictates on pure travel to consider, I paid extra to have an actual seat on the ferry instead of the deck, and boarded. Once I got settled, I decided I better take stock of my finances. I had about 140 pounds, which was close to $350 American. It wasn't a lot, but it wasn't time to panic.

By the time I took the ferry from Dublin to Manchester, caught the train to London, stayed in my old hostel for two days, got souvenirs and mailed them back home, then bought the rail pass that would allow me to travel between countries for the rest of the year, it was getting close to time to panic.

When I got on the train to Munich, I was surprised to see the majority of travelers were young people with a pack, and many resembled my hippie friends. I steered clear of them, but made friends with a German girl named Tildie. I was putting my backpack on the floor and noticed the shiniest pair of shoes I had ever seen before. It made me think of my cousin Caroline and how she had dumped rootbeer on her boyfriend Alton's shoes because he hadn't shined them to suit her. She'd sure like this fellow, I thought. I looked into the aisle, following the man the shoes belonged to. Yep, she'd like him. He was tall and slender and looked like he had just stepped off a movie set. Maybe out of a John Wayne movie. Even though he was dressed in a suit, something about him looked rugged, like he'd feel more comfortable in a pair of jeans and boots. I'd like to take him back to Hot Coffee, but even if I could, Caroline had already married poor old Alton.

I realized that Tildie was talking to me and pulled my attention away from Cowboy Man. Tildie and I talked non-stop from London to Paris, where we had to change trains in midafternoon for the second leg of the trip. I wonder why they call it legs? I'll have to look that up. Anyway, I told Tildie all about growing up in the South, and she kept calling my crazy relatives "cute."

I forgot all about Collins and the cute relatives when I stepped off the train in Paris at the Gare du Nord. The London train station was huge, but the Paris station was a work of art. I took a lot of pictures to show Mary Beth McClendon, my best friend back home. We used to go to the Collins Train Depot and watch the trains and dream about places we would go someday. But the Gare Du Nord made the Collins depot look like a tractor shed. There were these amazing sculptures, like it was a gallery instead of a train station. We couldn't stay long though. Tildie said we had to

194

walk to the Gare de L'Est to catch the train to Munich. Walking along Rue de Chabrol, we saw a little bistro and stopped for a quick lunch. By that time, I was telling her about my money woes and said I was going to have to look for a job and a place to stay in Munich.

"I work at a biergarten near the Marienplatz," said Tildie, "and I know a place, a *herberge*." I looked at her blankly. "A place to sleep. . . for young people," she tried. "It is not a lot of money."

"A hostel?" I asked hopefully.

"Yes," she said happily. "That is it. A hostel."

"Tildie," I cried suddenly, causing her to spill tomato gazpacho down her shirt. "We are in Paris."

"Yes." She nodded, dabbing at her blouse and looking at me warily like I might have Turret's or Alzheimers. "We are supposed to be in Paris, nein?"

"Well, yeah. But I mean it's just so amazing that I am actually in Paris, France, eating soup at a bistro."

"You don't like soup?" she asked.

"It isn't the soup. It's the fact that I am here at all. I've never been further than the Smoky Mountains in Tennessee. That's in the southern part of the United States," I clarified.

"Oh. Yes, I see," she said thoughtfully. Apparently that intrigued her as she then asked me a lot of questions about my life growing up and my experiences since I had been in Europe. She laughed when I told her about my family, and my time with the hippies, and nodded understandingly as I gushed on and on about all my dreams and plans. Then she went thoughtful again as I confessed how close to out of money I was and how totally unsure I was about what to do from here.

"I think perhaps I can help, Evangeline," she said. "The biergarten, it is very busy, especially with Oktoberfest. It was hard for me to get time to tend to business in London. Herr Diefenbach said he had not enough people and was angry that I insisted I must go. I think he would let you work if I promise him that I will teach you what to do."

"Oh, Tildie!" I cried. "You think so? Thank you. I didn't know what I was I was going to do. This is so sweet of you."

I didn't realize how worried I was until I felt the relief of Tildie's offer to help me find work and a place to stay. I was almost giddy. Of course, that might have been partly because of the Bordeaux she insisted on buying and sharing with me.

As we stood up to go back across the street to the station to catch what Tildie called the TGV, which was some kind of train, I asked, "Do you think we can see the Louvre from here?"

"Nein. But it is not far. In that direction." She pointed kind of to the left behind us.

On the way to Munich, Tildie wrote down the name of the hostel and drew a map for me so I could find my way from the train station. I didn't want to spend any of what I had left on buses or taxis since I didn't know how much the hostel would be. Besides, I had gotten pretty used to walking with my hippies. Tildie and I talked and talked, but as I was walking from the train to the hostel, I realized that while I had told her just about everything there was to know about me, I hadn't really learned much about her. She had told me about Herr Diefenbach and the beer garden, and she had some really funny stories about customers and the people she worked with, but she didn't really say anything personal about herself. I could kick myself. I must have been so self-absorbed, I didn't ask.

I found the hostel right near a tram stop, and it turns out it was a quick ride to the Marienplatz and Tildie's beer garden. Aunt Lavinia must have been doing double duty praying for me, as I got the last bed in the place. The girl at the counter said it was nearly impossible to get a room right in the middle of Oktoberfest, and it was almost miraculous that I had come in right when a girl had unexpectedly gotten called home. She had just checked out when I walked up.

My bed was in a room with five other girls; one of them, Nina, was an American from Minnesota. None of the others spoke English, so Nina and I bonded pretty quickly. She had plenty of money, so she didn't have to get a job, but we spent time together when I wasn't working at the beer garden. (Tildie had come through with the job.) Nina had been to Munich before and she showed me the zoo and some museums and gardens, and St. Peter's Church, and a lot of other things when I had time off. When I was working, I just fell into bed the minute I could get myself back to the hostel.

Tildie, after being so friendly and helpful on the train, didn't seem to want to pal around much once we got to Munich. She was older than me, but I had really thought we would become better friends. Still, she was nice, and she did talk Herr Diefenbach into hiring me and she helped me learn about serving in the beer garden, and communicating with the customers. I was learning some German, but the customers were from all over the world and I found that most could speak a little bit of English, so that made it easier. One day, I thought I saw Cowboy Man in the beer garden, but by the time I made my way through all the people, he was gone. If it even was him.

When I first got to Munich, everybody I met was talking about the October Fest. I figured it was kind of like the harvest festivals back home, but this was only the last week of September. When I went to the beer garden, I found out real quick the festival wasn't about October or harvest time. Apparently the Germans love beer so much they have a two-week party dedicated to the brew every fall. Maybe they should call it Steinfest. The only person I ever knew that dedicated to beer is Buddy Ray Pitts, back home in Collins. I guess he loves it even more. He has a year-round festival. If the pile of Dixie Beer cans behind his trailer was flattened out, he'd probably have enough metal to build an aircraft carrier.

I've never seen so many people in one place as at Oktoberfest, all drinking beer and eating sausage. There were tents everywhere, full of beer, schnapps, and food, and a lot of the men wore green leather shorts with suspenders and knee socks. Aunt Helen would get a kick out of that. There were rides like at the State Fair in Jackson. And music. I heard an American call it oompah music and there were bands with clarinets, tubas, flutes, and these weird instruments called mountain horns. Everybody there seemed really happy. But then again there *was* all that beer.

After the beer festival was over, Herr Diefenbach cut my hours. The hostel wasn't expensive and I had bought a kind of meal plan there, plus I was allowed to eat one meal at the beer garden the days I worked, so I wasn't spending a lot of money. But I needed to replenish my travel fund. I told Tildie one day that I might need to get a second job.

"This is funny," she said.

"Not to me," I retorted.

"No, not funny like laughing. Funny like it is strange you should say this to me today."

"Why is that?" I asked.

Tildie looked around before lowering her voice and answering, "Because just this day, a businessman I know asked if I could do some errands for him. I told him I was very busy, but he said he needed someone he could trust and he knows no other person that well in Munich," she said.

My ears perked up like a bird dog on point.

She continued. "He would pay well as he is very wealthy. I could tell him you are a trustworthy friend if you are interested."

"Shoot yeah, I'm interested," I said.

"Come to the Marienplatz tomorrow morning, to the Glockenspiel. You know it?"

"Yes," I answered. "My friend Nina took me there."

"You come. Nine O'clock. And don't bring your friend. The businessman, . . . umm. . . Heinrich, he would want you to be quiet about these errands. I think he wants to have delivered some very expensive things."

"Why doesn't he just do it himself?" I asked.

Tildie looked annoyed. "He is a very busy man. I must get back to work now. Bring your bag, your—what did you call it? Back pack?—tomorrow." Then she turned and hurried to a table where five people had just sat down.

I went to the Glockenspiel the next morning. A couple of minutes before nine, Tildie walked up carrying a shopping bag. "Is that. . ." I began, but she interrupted. "I must use the restroom." She motioned for me to follow her. Inside the bathroom, she took a music box out of the shopping bag and told me to put it in my backpack. Before I could ask why, she said it was a very expensive antique and she was afraid it would be stolen if anyone saw it. She gave me a slip of paper with the address of a book and gift store in Stuttgart. I was to go into the clock room at the back of the store and wait for a man who would be wearing a gray suit with a pink handkerchief in his pocket. If he was Gottfried, Tildie said, he would ask me if I liked clocks. I was to say I was really interested in the cuckoo clocks. He would then ask where I was from, and I was to say from the United States, but that I was living and working in Munich. That way we would each know who the other was for sure. Then I was to give the music box to Gottfried and he would give me an envelope with my pay in it.

"Gottfried is a friend of Heinrich," Tildie said, as if this explained everything. It seemed like an odd way to do business, but I wasn't familiar with foreigners, so I trusted Tildie. And I could sure use some extra money.

"Okay," I said. "What's this?" I asked as she held out a hand with a number of deutschemarks.

"You will need money for the train, yes?"

"No, I have a rail pass."

"Don't use it. Pay with this," she said.

"Well, okay," I agreed. It seemed like a waste of money, but nothing else made a lot of sense about this whole thing either. Germans sure weren't a trusting bunch.

We walked back out to the square, Tildie still holding the empty shopping bag. "Take the 11 o'clock train. If you do this well, there may be other deliveries to Gottfried. But tell no one, as Gottfried and Heinrich, they are afraid of the thievers."

I took the train, and in about two and a half hours I was in Stuttgart, looking for the store. It was not far from the station and I found it without any problem. I went into the clock room and looked around. A man came in, but before I could say anything to him, another man walked in. They were both wearing gray suits. Then an elderly couple came in apparently arguing about a figurine she was holding. They spoke German, so I didn't know what they said, but I think she was winning.

The mad couple left, then one of the gray suits left and the other came and stood looking at the same shelf I was looking at. He had a pink handkerchief in his coat pocket. I forgot everything Tildie had said and I asked, "Are you Gottfried? 'Cause if you are, I have a delivery for you." I took my pack off and started to open it, but the man that might or might not be Gottfried looked like I had said I had a box of cow brains for him, and motioned for me to stop. He looked around, then opened the door to what was apparently a store room and waved me inside. I took out the music box and handed it to him, and he almost grabbed it out of my hand. I was beginning to worry that he was one of the thievers Tildie warned me about, but then he said, "Gut. Danke," and handed me an envelope that seemed like it was way too fat. I was about to ask Gottfried about it, but he opened the door, looked around the clock room, then shooed me out of the storeroom, out of the clock room, and right out the door of the store.

"You're welcome," I muttered, then started walking back to the train station. I was really hungry, as it was midafternoon and I hadn't had any dinner. I guess I should call it lunch. It seems everybody outside Mississippi thinks dinner is at night. There was a little café a few blocks from the store and I sat down. A very large man brought me a menu and I started looking for anything that didn't end in *wurst*. It seemed liked everything I got the first week in Munich was some kind of sausage.

I ordered and as I waited for my leberkäse, I opened the envelope, and nearly swallowed my tongue when I saw all the marks in there. Gottfried must have made a mistake. I ordered a glass of wine (I didn't even get light headed anymore, although I drank wine with every meal except breakfast), and thought for a while. Maybe Gottfried meant to be paying for the music box and the delivery. But no, Tildie said it was very expensive, and even though the envelope had a lot of money in it, it wasn't enough to pay for some fancy antique. I would just have to talk to Tildie about it.

When my meal came out, I was relieved to see it was a meatloaf. The relief only lasted until the first forkful hit my tongue. Before I could think, I spit it right out on the table and took a big drink of wine. "Yuck. That's just like liver," I said to no one. I hated liver. I looked around for some ketchup to kill the taste.

"It is liver, Miss Tanner," said a deep voice behind me. I spun around and who was standing there but Cowboy Man. "Eat the kartoffelpuffer," he said.

"The what? And how do you know my name?"

"The potato pancakes. They are really good. Especially with applesauce. May I sit here?"

"I guess so," I said, and repeated, "How do you know me?"

Cowboy Man called the waiter over and ordered two pastries called obstkuchen before answering.

"My name is Daniel Overstreet and I am with the U.S. Embassy," he said. The obstkuchen came and he gave one to me and moved the plate with the liver meatloaf to the table next to us.

"I have reason to believe you may have placed yourself in an unfortunate situation."

"Why would the Embassy know whether or not I was in any situation, unfortunate or not?" I asked. Daniel Overstreet chewed on his apple pastry without answering and I just kept staring at him, nibbling on my own pastry. He had bright blue eyes that were kind of squinted like he spent a lot of time staring into the sun.

"You trust a German girl you barely know when she tells you to make a secret delivery, but you don't trust an American who tells you he is from the Embassy?"

When he put it that way, I began to question, but indignation won out over reason. "How do you know about, I mean, why would you think I was involved in any secret delivery?"

I remembered seeing Daniel, Cowboy Man, Overstreet on the train and in the beer garden. "Have you been spying on me?"

Cowboy Man swallowed, then sighed. "Well, as a matter of fact I have." He pulled a little wallet-like thing out of his pocket and shoved it at me. "I'm not with the Embassy. I'm with D.A.D., an American intelligence agency.

"Huh," I said, but I sat still and waited for him to continue. "Didn't you think it was suspicious that your friend, Tildie, asked you to come to Stuttgart and deliver a package?"

"No, I didn't. She has a friend in the antiques business and he needed somebody to deliver a valuable mu. . . item."

"Why didn't he just ship it then?" asked Cowboy Man, who was apparently Agent Overstreet. "And why all the secrecy? I bet she had a system worked out for you to recognize each other. Doesn't that seem suspicious to you?"

"Well, it didn't until now," I answered.

"Tildie, which isn't her real name by the way, is a spotter."

I nodded like I knew what that meant.

"She probably saw you were a naïve young girl who wouldn't arouse any suspicion and decided to use you as a mule."

"Now, wait a minute. Who are you calling a mule? And it was just a little music box, nothing that would require a mule."

"Miss Tanner, a mule is someone who is used to carry intelligence or drugs, an unwitting courier."

"Intelligence?" I perked right up and forgot all about my apple pastry. "I've been working with spies?"

"I am afraid so, Miss Tanner. I believe you've been used to carry film or documents concealed in that music box."

"How did you know it was a music box?" I asked suspiciously.

"You told me."

"Oh. I did, didn't I?" I could see I wasn't a very good spy. Even Uncle Cletus would have seen through me.

"I can't believe I fell for that," I said. I could imagine the whole framework of America falling. We would be using Russian rubles in no time and all because of me.

"Don't beat yourself up," Agent Overstreet said kindly. "You can turn this into an opportunity to help your country if you're willing."

"How?"

"Well, you can go back to Munich and tell your contact, Tildie, that everything went well and you would like to do it again if there is a need."

The mention of Tildie made me suspicious again. She was so good to me I just couldn't believe she was a spy, and I told Agent Overstreet that. He pulled out an envelope from a briefcase I hadn't even noticed he had with him, and showed me a picture of Tildie and some man in a uniform outside a shabby gray building that looked like it had been caught in the middle of a war.

"This was taken in East Berlin. The woman you know as Tildie is Nadia Meyer and the man is a Stasi officer. The Stasi are the East German secret police. We know that she was recruited by the Stasi and placed in Munich, but until now we haven't been able to find out what she was doing."

"You were on the train from London to Munich. I saw you," I said.

"I was following Nadia. Apparently, you have sharper eyes than she does. Lucky for me."

"It was your shoes," I said. "I've never seen a pair of shoes so shiny. I saw them. . . you. . . again in Munich. Where I work."

I thought for a minute, then said, "How can I help?"

"The next time Nadia asks you to make a delivery, you give us the package before you do the meet. We'll make a copy and then send you on your way."

I was getting excited. I, Vangie Tanner from Collins, Mississippi, was doing espionage. Or counter espionage. I wasn't sure of the distinction. I thought back to the episodes I had seen of The Man from U.N.C.L.E. "I know. If we agree to a drop, I'll go to St. Peter's Church and light three candles with a cigarette lighter. That will be the signal."

Agent Overstreet shook his head, sighed deeply, then handed me a card that said Denny Fischer with Munich Bus Tours. "Just call me at this number and say you want to take a tour and give me the date, time, and the city Nadia is sending you to. I'll have someone at the train station in Munich and I'll meet you somewhere along your route to the meet."

"How will you know what the route is?"

"That's my job, Miss Tanner. I'll find you."

I agreed and Agent Overstreet left, saying how nice it was to meet a fellow American and how he hoped I would have a good visit to Germany. I played along, figuring he was saying that for the benefit of the waiter or any spies that might be in the neighborhood.

I was almost as high as Cosmic River after a night smoking MJ. This was far out. Agent Overstreet was the man from DAD and I was the girl from UNCLE.

I SPY

I went straight to the beer garden, and asked if Gottfried had made a mistake with the money, but Tildie assured me it was the right amount. Money was no object to her friend. If I was interested, she said, I could make another delivery in a few days. I agreed and she said she would talk to Heinrich and let me know the details.

I walked back to the hostel, congratulating myself on my performance with Tildie. She didn't seem the least bit suspicious. When I got to my room, Nina was just going out, and I went with her and a couple of other people to the Hofbrauhaus. We got there and people were standing up with their arms linked swaying and singing. I figured the stout must have been flowing pretty freely, but soon we were swaying with the best of them. Our waitress could carry ten beer steins in each hand. I could carry four now, but I didn't know how she managed ten. These weren't tea glasses either. Buddy Ray Pitts could probably put three Dixie beers in one German stein. Maybe I should bring one of those beer steins back to him, but then I might be helping him along what Aunt Lavinia calls the broad path that leads to destruction. Although he was so far down that road already, I don't see what one beer glass would matter.

I had to work the next two days, but Tildie practically ignored me. I was beginning to wonder if I had blown my cover, maybe called her Nadia, or done something else equally stupid. But before I left work on Saturday night, she said to meet her at the Glockenspiel on Monday morning at ten. She wasn't a very imaginative spy, I thought. I would have chosen a different meeting place. Maybe worn a disguise.

I was in the Marienplatz at ten and just as the clocks began to chime, I felt a hand on my arm. I turned around and saw Tildie walking away. Again to the restroom. She gave me a figurine in a gift bag and told me to meet Gottfried in Stuttgart, but this time in a bakery. He would have a gift bag like mine. I was to sit down near the window by the front door, place the bag on the floor by the wall, and order a coffee. Gottfried would come in and sit right behind me and put his bag next to mine. Then he would take my bag, leave his in its place, and get up and get a pastry and leave. I would finish my coffee and then pick up the switched bag that would have my money in it and go back to the train and return to Munich.

I waited until I was in the train station, and after buying a ticket to Stuttgart, walked over and looked at some brochures for different tour companies. Just in case I was being tailed, I made a big show of asking a couple of people about one of the brochures then went to a pay phone and called the number on the card Agent Overstreet had given me. I had memorized the number and destroyed the card. I had planned to eat the card so there wouldn't be any evidence, but I kept remembering Mama always telling me not to put paper or money in my mouth since I didn't know where they had been, so I burned it instead.

When Cowboy Man answered, I told him I'd like to take a tour in Stuttgart the same afternoon and he said he would make the necessary arrangements. I took the train to Stuttgart, and when I got off, I was standing in front of this really tall tower with a Mercedes-Benz symbol on top. It was too early to meet Gottfried, and I was wondering what to do to kill time when this man bumped into me, nearly knocking me over. He grabbed my hand and steadied me, said something in German I took for an apology, then hurried on his way. But I could feel a little square of paper in my hand.

I went back into the train station to look for a powder room. The line was long, and I was about to rip a stitch I was so anxious to read that note. When I finally got in, I had to pay to use the toilet, but all that money Heinrich was paying me made that a small inconvenience. One thing about it, though, German bathrooms are so private, I didn't have to worry about witnesses. They aren't like the public bathrooms in America with their barely closed stalls. You get your own private little commode closet.

The note read, Statue of Count Eberhard the Bearded in Mittlerer Schlossgarten. I said it out loud seven times to sear it into my memory, then flushed the note down the toilet, opting for the big flush for security reasons. I then went back into the station and found a map to various tourist attractions, among them Mittlerer Schlossgarten. I found the statue and was looking up at it when Cowboy Man was suddenly standing beside me. He told me to give him the object Nadia had given to me, and he took the figurine and handed it to a man standing on the other side of him.

While pointing to the big statue of the count, he said softly. He's TSD."

"The Count?" I asked, confused.

Agent Overstreet just dipped his head in the direction of the man who took the figurine, then said, "Technical Services. He'll remove whatever is concealed, duplicate it, and put it back exactly as it was for you to deliver."

"Just the facts, ma'am," I said, but Cowboy Man didn't seem to appreciate my attempt at levity. In an unbelievably short time, the TSD man was back, and the figurine was sitting safely in its gift bag. Agent Overstreet suggested I also see the Oberer Schlossgarten, said it was nice to meet me, and walked away. I tipped my head forward in silent acknowledgment, feeling like I was getting pretty good at this spy thing. Walking along, trying to be sure I wasn't being shadowed, I was thinking of code names for myself. Before long I was at Bäckerei Treiber sitting by the window sipping coffee.

Just like Tildie said, Gottfreid came in, sat in front of me, switched bags, got a pastry and left. I bought an apfelkuchen and ate it and finished my coffee. I thought about Aunt Tiny while I ate the apple cake. She had three big apple trees and she made all kinds of apple stuff every year. Her fried apple fritters were just about the best thing I ever tasted, but these German apple pastries might give her fritters a run for their money. I wished I could mail one home to her. I got a little homesick thinking about her and the rest of my family, but I had to remember I had a job to do. My country was counting on me. I stood up, got my pack, threw my trash away, and walked to the train station to make my way back to Munich. I bought a Robert Ludlum book at a little shop in the train station and decided when I got back I would stay at the hostel and read instead of going out with Nina. This spy business was hard work.

Apparently the TSD man knew his stuff and Tildie and Heinrich had no idea the figurine had been tampered with, because the next day at the beer garden Nadia told me I had another delivery to make on Thursday. I thought that was a lot of spy stuff happening in a little bit of time and felt a kind of squeeze in the pit of my stomach. Tilde acted like normal, so I don't know why I felt uneasy.

After work, I was headed back to the hostel when a black sedan pulled up beside me. The door opened and two big hands reached out, grabbed me, and pulled me into the car. I tried to scream, but no sound came out. As the car sped away, I looked at the man beside me. He had blond hair and almost had to fold up to fit into the car. Before I could say anything, Blondie said, "Miss Tanner, Mr. Overstreet requested to see you."

"I'd call this a kidnapping, not an invitation," I said, anger replacing fear now. Although the mention of Cowboy Man made me feel better, I was still dubious about being snatched right off the street. "Well, he could have just told me," I said. "Let me out and I'll go call him. I'm tired right now and he can tell me on the phone about my next . . ."

Blondie, who looked like he ought to be a linebacker, put his hand over my mouth, effectively stifling the word, "assignment." He then put a finger to his lips before saying, "Mr. Overstreet is waiting in his office."

He kept looking up at the rearview mirror and after a minute I caught on. We were probably being tailed. And maybe the car was bugged. I was so excited I was almost wiggling in my seat. I couldn't wait to tell them back home. Then I realized. This was a covert mission. It was like the joke about the Baptist preacher who decided to play hooky on a Sunday to go golfing. He was playing the best golf of his life when an angel asked God, "Are you going to let this slide? Do something!" So God said, "Watch this." The pastor hit a 425-yard tee shot and the ball went in the hole for a double eagle. The angel asked, "Why did you reward him?" God just smiled and said, "Who is he gonna tell?"

I snickered a little and Agent Linebacker looked at me like my mind had snapped from the strain, so I looked out my window. After a little bit we passed a courtyard that I was sure I had seen earlier. A little while later I saw it again. We were going in circles. I was about to point that out, but just then I heard ringing coming from something that looked like a car battery with a telephone receiver on top. Blondie reached down and picked up the receiver. "Yeah?" he said. "Right." He tapped the driver and said "Safehouse." The driver, who looked more like a movie star than a secret agent, turned the car a sharp right onto Sendlinger Strasse. I had been shopping with Nina there and I recognized it. He didn't stop to shop, though. He kept right on driving until we were out in the country in a wooded area.

Movie Star agent pulled up to this little stone cottage, drove around behind it, and parked. Blondie opened his door and I slid over and nearly jumped out right behind him. "You sure this is the right place?" I asked, looking around at the little stone cottage.

We were standing on a stone path in a garden that would probably be some kind of something come spring. Agent Overstreet stepped out of the shadows and scared the Tom Thunder out of me. "Miss Tanner," he said. "Come with me, please."

We went in the back door of the cottage into a kitchen that looked like somebody's rosy cheeked little grandma ought to be in there baking cookies instead of housing secret agents and their kidnap victims. There was no gate, no guards, no bars on the windows. Not even a Doberman pinscher patrolling. It looked more like a place Hansel and Gretel might have lived than any safe house.

"What's going on, Agent Overstreet?" I asked. Now that the excitement was dying down some, I was getting annoyed again that these guys had yanked me off the street without even asking me. I had wanted to take a bath and read that book I bought in Stuttgart.

"Miss Tanner, you need to leave Munich," said Agent Overstreet.

"I'll be leaving soon," I said. "I want to do another mission or two so I'll have plenty of money when I leave."

"No, ma'am, you need to leave now. We'll take you wherever you want to go."

"Now! What do mean? Right now? This minute? I don't have my clothes or anything," I protested. "All I have is my handbag and this book. I took *The Osterman Weekend* out of my bag. "I was going to read. . ."

"Your personal belongings will be sent to you," interrupted Agent Overstreet. "Are you paid up at the hostel?"

"Well, yes, I pay them every Saturday for the upcoming week."

"Okay." He thought for a minute. "Where do you want to go?"

"I was planning to go to Paris next," I said, "but I can't just leave my job without even giving notice."

"Miss Tanner, your life is in danger. You have to leave Munich tonight. This is not a game," he said before I could protest further.

"You mean my cover is blown?" I whispered. Agent Overstreet sighed.

"We'll escort you to Paris, and we'll take care of your hostel. You write a note explaining that you had an emergency and had to go home. Don't say where home is. We'll send your belongings to you. You can't go back to Munich. Do you understand?"

I was beginning to understand all too clearly. I wasn't Agent Illya Kuryakin. I was Evangeline Tanner and spies wanted me gone. Or dead. Spying didn't seem like nearly as much fun all of a sudden.

"They want to kill me?" I said, my lip trembling a little.

"Maybe you should think about going back to the states, to your family," said Agent Overstreet. "Whatever you want, but you can't go back to the hostel."

"I don't want to go home," I finally said. "I want to see Paris."

Agent Overstreet took my arm and walked toward the door, Blondie and Movie Star driver right behind. We all got in the car and Agent Overstreet called somebody on the car battery thing. I guess the car wasn't bugged because he wasn't talking in code or anything. He said something to the driver and got in the back seat with me. Blondie got in on the other side of me and boom, just like that I was on my way out of Germany and out of the spy business.

I was thankful I carried all my money with me all the time. At least I wouldn't be dropped off in Paris dead broke. We drove most of the night. I woke up when the car stopped and I found I had fallen asleep with my head on Agent Linebacker's shoulder. I think I drooled onto his suit coat. We were in front of a big hotel. Agent Overstreet went in, then came back out a few minutes later and said he had a room for me. I could stay at the hotel for a week "on the U.S" he said, during which time all my stuff from Munich would be sent to my room. After that, I was on my own, although he did say to call him at the number on the card he had given me if I needed him. I had to confess that I had burned the card, but he gave me another one. This one had another number, handwritten on the back.

"The number on the back is the field office in Paris. If you see Nadia or anyone suspicious, or you get any strange phone calls, anything that worries you, you call that number."

I squared my shoulders, took a deep breath, and nodded. Agent Overstreet walked me into the hotel and saw me to the elevator and handed me a room key and a bunch of francs. I took it all in my left hand, then stuck my right hand out, trying to keep it steady. Agent Overstreet shook my hand and said, "It's been a pleasure working with you, Miss Tanner."

My room was a lot nicer than the hostel, but it wasn't fancy. I mean it didn't have a marble bathroom and stone fireplace like the one I had read about in a brochure back in Munich. I guess the government doesn't pay secret agents all that well. I sat on the bed and thought about the past few weeks and my experiences in the spy business. I didn't know if I had the guts to do it again, but at least I could get a job as a waitress when I got home. I was up to seven beer steins in each hand now.

Again, I sort through the pile of European mementoes and hold up a brass miniature of the Eiffel Tower. Paris. It took less than a week for Paris to point me toward my certain future. Still holding the miniature, I notice an unstamped envelope, and I pull from it a few folded pages of hotel stationery covered with my own writing. A letter to Aunt Helen,

November 15, 1973

Dear Aunt Helen,

As you well know, I've been planning my first day in Paris for years and now that I am actually here, I am spending my first day hiding in a hotel room, listening for the footsteps of the spies that will surely be coming to kill me. I didn't wake up until eleven (espionage is exhausting), and I spent the next hour debating whether I should go shop for clothes or just take a shower and put back on the same dirty clothes I've worn and slept in for more than twenty-four hours. Agent Overstreet, he's like the head guy from UNCLE, remember that show? Or maybe you don't since you don't pay much attention to the TV. Anyway, he's my contact in the CIA, and he kidnapped me from Germany and plopped me down in a hotel in Paris to save my life from Russian spies. He told me I could get a toothbrush and toothpaste from the front desk, and I did, but no way was I going to ask if they had a stash of clean underwear.

I finally just gave up on the whole thing. I am afraid if I get in the shower, that's when Tildie AKA Nadia will bust down the door and there I'll be, running for my life through the streets of Paris in my altogether. I am hungry, too, but I am afraid to leave the room.

I took French my junior year, so I am going to watch television and see if I can understand any of it. I need to try to take my mind off everything.

6 p.m.

I am not only still scared and hungry, I am now naked, except for a robe the hotel had laying across the bed. I remembered you and Aunt Tiny telling me how y'all used to have to wash clothes in a Number Two galvanized tub with a wash board, so I figured I could find a way to make do. I put my clothes in the bathtub, then got in and swished them around with my feet, trying to make motions like a washing machine agitator. I wrung them out as well as I could and hung them over the shower rod to dry.

It is getting dark and no door busting has been forthcoming so far, and I am beginning to feel a little better. I have been sitting propped up in the bed watching French television, but I could only pick out a few words every now and then, so I've been imagining myself as a reclusive movie star, holed up in France to get away from my adoring fans for a little while. You know what? A movie star wouldn't allow herself to go hungry, reclusive or not. She'd just call room service and order something elegant. So that's what I am going to do. I am sure the United States of America wouldn't want me to starve to death. I wonder how long I can stay in this room before the hotel kicks me out.

November 16, 1973
7 a.m.

I went to bed early after I got my food from room service. I had to sleep au naturale since my clothes were still pretty wet. I was so exhausted, I slept like a hound dog fresh off a hunt, and

I'm feeling a little better. I just have to decide what to do next. The first step is to actually leave this room and the second ought to be to find some more clothes. Washing clothes in a bath tub is not a hobby I want to take on. Ha ha.

6:30 p.m.

My clothes weren't completely dry, but I put them on anyway and went downstairs and found a café right next door to the hotel. By the time I had finished a café au lait (that's strong coffee with hot milk) and a chocolate croissant, I had quit looking around for spies altogether. Have you ever had a chocolate croissant? I can't even describe it. It's kind of like a Danish, but lighter and richer, and it has this chocolate inside that would make Mrs. Brewer throw her chocolate cream pie out the window in shame.

I needed to shop, but what I wanted to do was go to the Louvre first. I mean, what if somebody dropped the big one while I was picking out panties without ever seeing the Mona Lisa? I asked the girl at the counter for directions and it turned out I was just around the corner from it. In no time I was standing in front of this amazing building. Aunt Helen, it looked like a castle, not an art museum. Of course, that's kind of what it was in the 1300s. I think it was a fort or something before that. It's weird to even say the words "before 1300." Back home, ancient history is anything before 1910!

When I walked in the main doors, I was smashed in with wall-to-wall people. This was more crowded than the beer garden during Oktoberfest, and that's way worse than the biggest day at the State Fair in Jackson. Remember that time you wanted to go to the fair and Daddy and I took you and you got panicky when you felt all those people pushing and shoving? I think I understand how you felt. I can see, but I still felt almost like I was being pushed along with no control and no way out.

I had a map they gave me with my ticket and when I could manage to look at it, I figured out real quick that a day here isn't even going to get me started. There are thousands of things I want to see; there are paintings floor to ceiling. You wouldn't believe it. But you know what I wanted to see first. Me and just about everybody in France, it seemed. I had to wait forever to get close enough to really see it. Some things in other rooms caught my eye, like this one sculpture in the Egyptian exhibit that looked just like Mr. Spock on Star Trek, but I kept moving. Along the way I saw a lot of stuff. I mean a lot of stuff.

And then, there I was. Standing right in front of her. The Mona Lisa. You know, it is a lot smaller than I always thought. I slapped my leg to be sure I was really in Paris looking at a painting by Leonardo Da Vinci and not just having a hallucination from all the MJ smoke I breathed back in Ireland with the hippies. Unfortunately, I also slapped the man next to me and had to apologize. He sniffed and muttered under his breath and moved as far away as the crush of people would let him. I sure wish Jamie was here with me. I miss him a lot, Aunt Helen.

I finally made myself leave Mona Lisa, and made my way to the Dutch exhibit. I understand now why Jamie loves Vermeer and Rembrandt so much. I have seen pictures of some of the paintings, but to be there and see them for myself was totally different. I wish you could see them. I could hardly breathe. I know you'll understand when I say that I feel like it is a revelation of my calling. The muse speaking to me, you know? I decided that when I left I would go straight to an art store and buy some pencils and a sketch pad. I didn't want to waste another minute neglecting my gift.

I spent all day at the Louvre and now I am in a restaurant. I feel stupefied, like I gorged on art and my mind can't digest it all. Almost an art coma. Now I guess I'll add food coma to that. I couldn't read the menu, so I ordered steak au pouivre, because I at least know what steak is, and some kind of salad. Oh, here it comes now. I'll finish this back at the hotel.

9 p.m.

When I got back to my hotel, all the things I left behind in Munich were there in the room waiting for me. Good thing, too, because I completely forgot about shopping. No playing washing machine agitator tonight. Yippee!!! I thought about calling Cowboy Man to thank him, but decided it might not be such a good idea.

My supper was really good, Aunt Helen. The steak had some kind of pepper sauce and it was amazing. The salad wasn't anything like Mrs. Cowan's seven-layer salad or even Aunt Tiny's tossed greens. It had green and purple lettuce. Did you know there was purple lettuce? And it had oranges and cranberries in it and something called Chèvre, that tasted like cheese that was about to turn, with this dressing they called vinaigrette. I thought it would be sour, but it wasn't. It sure wasn't Thousand Island, but it was good. Even the old cheese was good after a couple of bites to get used to it. When the waiter brought a dessert menu, I just pointed to something and hoped for the best. It turned out to be some kind of raspberry cake.

I have on clean dry pajamas now and I climbed in bed to read, but my book, The Osterman Weekend, is a little too close to home, so I decided to finish my letter to you. I am going back to the Louvre tomorrow. I plan to be out the door by eight in the morning. Any later, as Daddy always says, and I'll be burning daylight.

November 20, 1973

I haven't written because I've been exploring the Louvre for the last three days. When I get back to the room after supper every day, I am so filled up, and not with the food, that I can't do anything but get in my PJs and just think about it all. It is almost like going to a revival back home. I feel like running to the altar and rededicating my life, but to being an artist. Aunt Lavinia would think I am being sacrilegious, but I'm really not. It feels like a spiritual thing. Aunt Helen, I know exactly what I want to do with my life. As soon as I get back home, I am enrolling in college in Hattiesburg to study art. I am going to paint. It's my destiny.

Something odd happened today. I kept seeing this man everywhere I went in the Louvre. With all the people, it's hard to break out of the stream, but it seemed like he was trying to keep up with me. When I looked straight on at him, he would look away and investigate a painting or something. It didn't feel right and I remembered how I had told Tildie about how much I wanted to come to Paris and see the Louvre. I didn't mention to Agent Overstreet that I had told her that. I didn't even think about it until today.

When the crowd passed a bathroom, I ducked inside real quick and when I came out, I walked behind this really fat lady, staying right up close to her until I was a good way away. When I looked back, the man was standing near the bathroom door, apparently studying an exhibit near it. I was pretty sure then that he was following me, so I made my way out of the museum and hightailed it back to the hotel. I'm not going back to the Louvre. If I see that man again, I'm going straight to a phone and call the number Agent Overstreet gave me.

I can't wait to see and talk to you for real, Aunt Helen. I love you. I only wish I could really mail this letter, but I can't tell even you about the spy stuff, and I certainly can't have Linda Sue, the Blabbermouth of the South, reading it to you.
All my love,
Evangeline

Of course, no one ever saw the letter. In fact, I recall thinking I should burn it so there would be no security breach, but instead I had tucked it in my backpack and eventually it landed in the Memory Box with my European memorabilia. As I hold the letter now, I remember the absolute certainty of my meeting with the muse in The Louvre. And I remember what followed.

THE MUSE

It was my sixth day in Paris, and I decided it was time to really get those art supplies and start painting or at least drawing. All the great artists went to Europe to paint and I was already here, so I needed to make the most of it. The girl at the front desk—she's just a fount of knowledge—said to go to the St. Germaine des prés area. She said it has a lot of shops of all kinds and the Ecole des Beaux Arts is there, where a bunch of the most famous artists, like Degas, Monet, and Renoir studied.

I hadn't seen the weird man from the Louvre, so either I lost him or he was never following me to begin with. Just to be on the safe side, I had stayed in the hotel room the whole next day, but since nothing happened I figured it was safe to go back out. I would just stay away from the art galleries, since that's what I had told Tildie I was interested in.

While I was walking, I saw bookstore after bookstore and decided to replace my Robert Ludlum with something that wouldn't remind me of my brush with death. I went in this one store and there was an American girl in there, wearing a beret and carrying a big cloth bag. I knew she was American because I heard her talking to a boy.

"Did you know Gertrude Stein lived here?" she said to him.

"Here? In this store?"

She hit his arm with a book. "Here, in Paris, moron."

"Yes, I do know that," he answered. "And I also know that she helped other writers, like Ernest Hemingway. . ."

"And F. Scott Fitzgerald, and Sherwood Anderson," the girl interrupted with a saucy toss of her head.

I had never heard of Sherwood Anderson. I moved a little closer, fascinated by their conversation, and drawn by their comfortingly familiar accent. Southerners both.

"Sometimes I think about staying here and writing. I could be an expatriate," she said then.

"An ex-patriot?" I asked right out loud, shocked. I almost wanted to put my hand over my heart and sing The Star Spangled Banner. I felt my face get hot when the two turned to stare at me. "I'm sorry," I said. "I was just so interested in hearing about those writers. But then when you said you didn't want to be patriotic anymore."

The girl looked at me a minute, then laughed. "No, I said expatriate," she said. "Like this." She took a piece of paper and a pen out of her bag and wrote expatriate on it. "It's just someone who lives outside their own country. A lot of writers did that. I think it would be glamorous."

"Glamorous," I repeated.

"My name is Gwen," she said then, "and this is Randy."

Randy stuck out his hand and I shook it. "I'm Evangeline," I said.

"You new to Paris?" Gwen asked.

"Yes, I just got here a few days ago. I've been traveling around and had to leave. . . " I hesitated a minute before finishing, ". . . Ireland when my friends went home. I decided to come to France and then I'll be going to Spain and Italy and maybe Austria and Switzerland and G-Germany." I didn't want to sound like I was avoiding Germany, but I didn't think I wanted to advertise that I had just been there either.

"What have you seen so far?" asked Randy.

"I spent the first few days seeing the Louvre."

"The Louvre," cooed Gwen. "It's fantastic, isn't it?"

I nodded.

"And now you're in literary heaven," she added. "Did you know there were hundreds of expatriate writers who lived here? James Baldwin, Richard Wright, James Joyce, Tod Anderson, T.S. Elliott."

Randy added, "William Burroughs wrote *Naked Lunch* here. Look." He put a pamphlet he was holding on the table where we had sat down. "This is a map of a walking tour of St. Germain des prés." He started pointing out places where famous writers had either spoken or lived or met. I didn't even know a lot of the names he was talking about.

"Why are y'all in Paris?" I asked when he stopped to take a breath.

"We're in a study abroad program," he said. "Studying literature," he added, although I could have pretty much guessed that. "We go to Emory in Atlanta, and we're here for the fall semester."

Randy went right back to naming off famous writers who had lived in Paris. "Do you know right here on Rue Mazet, George Sand smoked cigars with Flaubert, Gautier, and Turgenev?"

I nodded, but the only familiar word in that sentence was cigar. "When do you go back home?" I asked.

"December," Randy said and at the same time, Gwen answered, "I don't think I'm going back."

"What?" Randy said.

"I just told you I want to stay and write. I want to live here. It's wonderful."

It looked like there was about to be a fight, so I said, "Nice to meet you," and walked over to look for a book, still holding onto that map of the area. As I thought of all the famous people who came here to write, I began to feel that same altar call I had felt at the Louvre. I bought a copy of *The Crystal Cave* by this woman named Mary Stewart. It was about Merlin and King Arthur and I figured it would help me forget about spies and stuff.

I left the book store and saw a place called Café Procope. I looked at the brochure Randy had given me and learned it was built in 1686 and is the city's oldest café. Voltaire, Rousseau, the Marquis de Sade, Beaumarchais, Balzac, Verlaine, Hugo, La Fontaine, and Anatole France were all customers there at one time or another. I decided to eat lunch and see if I could feel any of their spirits. The food was amazing and there were some historic things, like Voltaire's marble desk and a letter from Marie-Antoinette.

After lunch, I followed the map and it was just place after place where famous writers had been or lived or worked. A lot of them I had never heard of, but I got a shiver just the same thinking that they had once walked these very streets I was walking. Street after street, house after house, the map showed where writer upon writer upon writer used to live. I swear I felt the muse calling and I got so confused wondering if I was supposed to be a writer or an artist that I asked for a sign. Like Gideon's fleece I learned about in Sunday School. Right after I said the words, "Send me a sign," I saw no. 60 Rue de Seine, the Hôtel La Louisiane. It was my answer. Mississippi. Louisiana. Hello. I was meant to be a writer for sure. I would follow in the footsteps of Gertrude Stein and Ernest Hemingway. I would be one with James Baldwin and Richard Wright, even though I was white. And a woman.

I was walking along thinking and when I looked up I realized that I was right near the main entrance of the Louvre. I was so startled I dropped my book on the sidewalk. Wham! I bent down to pick it up and when I stood up, who did I see staring at me but that same man who was following me two days before. What kind of karma was this, I wondered and hurried away waving and calling, pretending like I had seen a friend and was trying to catch up to them. I managed to get on a bus just as the man turned the corner after me and I sank down in the seat shaking like kudzu in a windstorm. Now what? I didn't think the spies knew where I was staying since I had only seen that one and I had only seen him at the Louvre, so I made my way back to the hotel and packed up my things. When I told the girl at the desk that I was checking out, she said I still had another night paid for. I said thanks, but I needed to get back home for a family emergency. To Little Rock, I added—just in case the spies came asking.

I went to a pay phone and pulled out the card. I had to leave Paris. I would a whole lot rather be back in Mississippi eating peas and cornbread, than smacking down chateaubriand in a fancy hotel with a pack of killer spies always on my tail. I didn't know if I would ever come back to paint or write, but right then I didn't care. I just wanted to sit on my own couch looking across the room into my Daddy's face. I just wanted to feel safe.

I was so relieved when Agent Overstreet himself came to pick me up I could almost have cried, but then relief began to mingle with anger and indignation over how a bunch of spies were running me right out of my dream of Europe. I met Agent Overstreet at the same bookstore where I had gotten to know Randy and Gwen, and he took me to the airport and put me on a plane bound for Jackson, Miss.

When I got home, I told everyone that Jamie didn't want me traveling in Europe without him, so I cut my trip short. I don't think Daddy bought it, but Aunt Lavinia would have lit a candle and said a Novena if the Baptists allowed it. She thought I was preparing to become a dutiful, obedient wife.

I didn't explain. I couldn't, but I spent a lot of time staring across the room at my Daddy in the following days, to the point where he said I was giving him the willies, so I had to remember to try and act normal.

As I reach toward the box again, I notice the clock on the bedside table. I have no more time. My flight leaves in six hours and I haven't even finished packing. Almost unseeing, I gather all the mementoes I have laid around the bed and replace them in their little shelter. I put the lid back on the Whitman Sampler box, sealing in my history, preserving my past. I think about taking the box with me, but decide to leave it here in this house, in this room. This part of me belongs in Covington County, Mississippi. I shove it back into the far corner of the dark closet, back into another life. I will be back in three months. Maybe then, I will be ready to revisit what brought me to where I am now. Then I notice on the floor a single blue dried flower and I am transported to one last memory.

It will be Dutch

"Stop that damn blubbering, Lavinia." Aunt Helen was in rare form today. I suspected she was nervous, but it came out as bad tempered. Aunt Lavinia, in her turn, was in an absolute frenzy of conflicting emotions. It was a big day for her, so I tried to deflect Aunt Helen by asking her to make sure Uncle Cletus had taken off the lizard-skin boots and put on the dress shoes I had shined for him the night before.

At that moment a wail erupted from the kitchen. "Just call the whole thing off," Aunt Lavinia cried, as I walked in to see what was wrong. "I can't have all them people in here expecting to eat and this blasted puddin' like a big tub of wallpaper paste. Why do they call it puddin'? There is nary a drop of sugar in the whole mess. And why would anybody eat puddin' of any descriptive with a roast beef anyway? A roast is supposed to be cooked in gravy with potatoes." Then guilt-stricken, she looked at me and began to sob in earnest. "I am sorry, Lamb," she blubbered. "I know you had your heart set on this fancy English cuisinart, but I swanee, I don't know a soul what'll eat it."

"It doesn't matter," I began, but Daddy, who had heard from upstairs came into the kitchen and took charge.

"Vangie, I'll take care of it. You just go get dressed." He patted my head, letting his hand linger on my hair for a moment before he turned to the task at hand. Conflictingly relieved and reluctant, I turned toward the stairs. "Just make a washtub of that lime jello mess and a big bowl of potato salad," I heard him say before his calming voice was reduced to a warm murmur. But I heard Aunt Lavinia laugh a moment later, so I knew he would make it alright.

I don't know why everybody was in such a stir. Everything had been planned for weeks, and the house was spit shined and filled with flowers. I think Jamie had bought out every florist in the country trying to obtain true blue flowers because blue is my favorite color. Daddy tried to make Jamie let him get the flowers, but Jamie refused to relinquish the task. I think he believed if anyone else did it, it would come short of being perfect for me. What the silly boy obviously didn't know was that everything was already perfect and that is why I was absolutely calm, sure, and blissful on this day when every Tanner and Tanner relation seemed to be coming apart at the seams.

Draped across the chenille bedspread in my room was the lacy white dress, slightly yellowed now, that Mama had saved for years. It really didn't fit me right and Mama wasn't here to know if I wore it or not, but I just had to. A small movement in the corner, maybe the slight shiver of the lace sheers on the windows in response to the soft spring breeze, made me wonder for a moment if maybe she were here after all. I really hadn't squared away the whole religious, spiritual question, so—just in case—I figured I better answer. I walked slowly over to the corner and stood beside the fluttering sheer panels. "Mama," I said, and unexpectedly my throat felt almost like it did the time Willie T sent a line drive right into my throat when we were playing softball in Uncle Brantley's back pasture. Just like then, the tears coursed upward and outward and down my face, but this time in rivers of loss and regret and a pain that doesn't heal with a bag of ice and soft pillow. It dims and mellows, then jumps up and stabs deep and raw and fresh. "Oh, Mama," I murmured when I could speak again. I swear to you, one of those panels blew softly over my face, blotting tears and softly caressing my cheek. Call it supernatural, call it a spring breeze, call it a flight of fancy. Whatever it was, the storm passed, and the calm returned, and I knew Mama would be standing right by Daddy watching her baby girl walk into the love she had always imagined for me.

I ran a bubble bath in the deep, claw-foot tub and poured in a bit of the lavender concoction that Mamie Hawkins had brought by two days before. Even though I didn't feel nervous now, it couldn't hurt to do a little preventive maintenance. As I luxuriated in the silky water, I anticipated the day ahead, the weeks ahead, the years ahead. Everything was right with Jamie. It had been since the day he brought me a glass of ice tea at Sandy's Fish House. Oh, we had had our bumps in the road. I was impulsive and full of the desire for grand adventures and he had to reel me in a few times. But more often, he just gave me that big smile and found a way to help me do whatever I had dreamed up.

I was starting college in the fall, finally getting on the path that had been set for me two summers before. As I began to float into dreams of the future, my reverie was stopped short like a bird flying into a fresh washed window pane. "My god, I look like a giant blueberry," came ringing out from somewhere down the hall.

"You look fine, Tiny, and don't take the Lord's name in vain," admonished Aunt Lavinia.

"A blueberry with a tiny little head," Aunt Tiny continued at increasing volume. "Why didn't anybody tell me?"

I got out of the tub and tied the fluffy white terry cloth robe around me and peered out into the hallway. Dressed in a clingy chiffon dress that was indeed the exact shade of that particular fruit, Aunt Tiny did look remarkably like one of the Fruit of the Loom guys. I stifled the giggles that threatened as Aunt Helen said, "Maybe it's not so bad. Come here and let me feel it."

"What can you tell about anything, by . . . Helen! Get your hands off my rear end." At this, everybody but poor Aunt Tiny was in near hysterics. She sniffed, turned and marched into Daddy's room and slammed the door. She insisted that Uncle Brantley take her home and when she finally returned two hours later, she was dressed in last year's Easter outfit with the black-

and-yellow striped skirt and sunshine yellow jacket. No one had the heart to tell her she now looked like a well-fed bumble bee.

By five o'clock, the dining room was set with a beautiful standing rib roast surrounded by, not Yorkshire pudding, but mounds of mustard-rich potato salad. The cliché lime jello mold was indeed in its place of honor on Mama's tea cart. A beautiful cake festooned with rope icing and pearls held court in the center of the buffet, flanked by the ancient cut-glass punch bowl filled with some nameless pink punch. Aunt Lavinia had tried for a week to come up with blue punch that didn't taste like bilge water and had finally settled for "coordinating pink." Family and friends were outside in the big backyard settling into metal folding chairs borrowed from Crossroads Missionary Baptist Church. That institution had come up in the world enough to have a for-real fellowship hall for homecoming and other events. I personally thought the relinquishing of plywood tables and blankets on the ground was a loss, not a gain.

I stood looking out the back door watching for Aunt Lavinia's signal to walk down the "aisle" designated by a generous sprinkling of cotton-candy-pink rose petals from Mama's earliest blooming climber. Daddy turned to look at me and smiled a bittersweet smile, nodding slightly. My stomach knotted up so I could barely breathe and I started having heart palpitations. I didn't want to have a heart attack right there in the backyard before I could become Mrs. Jamie Derrickson, so I turned to old ways and grabbed down the *World Book*, letter H, from the shelf in the living room. I ran back into the kitchen and was swallowing an aspirin to help my blood flow, when Aunt Lavinia came in in a panic. "It's time, Vangie, don't you hear the music?" In truth, all I could hear was the blood swirling around in my head and beating staccato in my ears. I think I should have stayed in the lavender bath a little longer.

Aunt Lavinia ushered me out the door, and Daddy offered his arm and began to walk me toward the old arbor already blooming out with yellow jasmine and with a fragrance like Heaven surely must smell. The moment I saw Jamie's brown eyes looking into mine, as Daddy placed my hand into his, a soft sense of right settled my blood, my heart, and my days to come. I might never be a Proverbs 31 wife, but I was about to be Jamie's.

Seriously short on time, now, I lay the flower on the bedside table and turn on the shower. When I am dressed in one of the trademark flowing skirts and organic cotton shirts that have become almost a uniform for me, I pack my suitcase and replace the folding easel and paint box into their travel case. While Jamie is by far the better artist, I have achieved a measure of success with my watercolors. I travel a good bit with shows and week-long painting clinics. Of course, it helps that the Agency has connections everywhere, allowing me to bypass the normal slow track to success. I am being picked up in ten minutes for the two-hour trip to Jackson, where I will catch a flight to Buenos Aires.

I bring my luggage downstairs, to Aunt Lavinia's dismay. "Why didn't you ask your Uncle Calvin to get those, Lamb? That kind of work is for men, not ladies." I don't mention the heavy lifting she does daily, nor the fact that Uncle Calvin is pushing eighty, nor the fact that the suitcases don't come close to what I regularly lift at the gym.

When the simple black sedan pulls into the drive and stops near the house, I mollify Aunt Lavinia by allowing Uncle Calvin and Uncle Cletus to each put a bag into the trunk. Uncle Calvin returns to the porch, but Uncle Cletus follows me to the passenger door, eying the car with speculation and deep suspicion. His eyes widen when I allow him to see the tip of the handle of the nine-millimeter Glock peeking from the holster clipped to the waistband of my skirt. Everyone is inured to his paranoid ramblings, so no harm can come of tossing him this particular bone. I wink, then readjust the loose-fitting peasant-style blouse I've chosen for more practical reasons than its suitability to my cover as an artist.

A Bohemian artist, I think, patting Uncle Cletus's arm. Although not quite rich and famous.

I wave to everyone one last time, then get in the passenger side and close the door. Uncle Cletus is dog tracking back to the safety of the house, his eyes never leaving the car with its deeply tinted windows.

My best friend in all the world, Special Agent Willie T. Clifford, my partner, tunes the radio to a rock station and turns the volume to near ear-splitting before getting right to business. "This extraction isn't going to be as simple as we thought," he says, leaning toward me so I can hear. He holds out a thick manila folder with pumpkin colored rubber bands around it, while expertly backing the car down the drive with his left hand. "There are some complications . . ."

I interrupt. I am not quite ready to leave behind the pleasant, relatively uncomplicated past in which I have immersed myself the past two days, so I circumvent the informal briefing with a version of my life mantra. Agent Clifford looks like he's chewing live lobsters when I say, "The trouble with extractions, Willie T, is the same as the trouble with grits . . ."

Phyllis Pittman

About the Author

 **Phyllis Pittman**'s career as a writer began with an attempt to publish a short story in the New Orleans *Times Picayune* newspaper at the age of nine. That ill-fated effort was followed some twenty years later by a career as a newspaper journalist, feature writer and columnist.

Her first published work of fiction was a children's book, *Pony Tales: Night Mischief,* published by SBA Books in 2014. She was co-author of two books with the Fairhope Writers Group: *Fairhope Anthology: Second in a Series*, and *Original Fairhope Guidebook: A Walking Tour in 2017.*

The Trouble with Grits, her debut novel, was a finalist in the 2017 William Faulkner/William Wisdom Writing Competition.

Born in Hattiesburg, Miss., Phyllis Pittman lives in Fairhope, Alabama, pursuing fiction writing full-time.

Made in the USA
Columbia, SC
10 June 2022